NIOMIE ROLAND

Jessa&Jaxon

Sweet, Steamy & Suspenseful
Romance

Contents

Prologue   1

Jaxon   11

Jessa   15

Jaxon   22

Jessa   26

Jaxon   30

Jessa   33

Jaxon   38

Jessa   43

Jaxon   49

Jessa   54

Jaxon   60

Jaxon   63

Jaxon   69

Jessa   73

Epilogue   78

Other Books By The Author   82

Prologue

efore their plans started falling apart, Meesha had turned to Jessa as they were sitting on one of the beds in their suite, picking out clothes for their night last night in Vegas.

"Can I ask you girls something?" Meesha asked, though her head was still bent staring at the silk blouse in her hand. She suddenly seemed to enjoy looking at it more than her friends.

Meesha was one of Jessa's closest friends in the world, next to Jasmine. Meesha was the reason for this Vegas trip. It was her bachelorette weekend. Though the wedding was still three months away, the girls wanted to visit Vegas during spring break since Jessa was a teacher and had the time off.

Jessa, along with her other best friend Jasmine stopped what they were doing and faced Meesha. "Girl, do you even have to ask? You can ask us anything."

"Just wanted to make sure," Meesha said as the corners of her lips turned up, then her smile wavered. "Do you girls feel like Connor and I are rushing things?" She asked while her hand once again trailed over the silk shirt.

Jessa and Jasmine looked at each other with widening eyes and raised eyebrows. They then turned concerned eyes toward their friend. Jessa could see the seriousness of Meesha's expression. She opened her mouth to respond, then closed it again. She started to say something again, but Jasmine spoke up before she could.

"It doesn't matter what we think. What do you think?" Jasmine asked. Her voice was calm, cool and collected.

"I don't know." Meesha shrugged, letting the skirt slip to the bed. "I just feel like there is a lot I haven't done, a lot I'm going to miss out on. I've been with him since forever. He was my first everything and I can't help feeling like I'm missing out on something. A chance to test out the waters," Meesha said in one breath.

Jessa did not understand her friend's dilemma. It was absolutely true that Connor and Meesha had been together for almost ten years. Since Meesha was fifteen and Connor was seventeen. Jessa however wished she had what Connor and Meesha had together. She did not fathom the reason for her friend's sudden bout of jitters.

"Girl, you don't know what you're –" Jessa did not get a chance to finish since Meesha's phone rang. She watched as her friend rummaged through her purse until she located it.

"It's Connor," she whispered to the girls and then placed the phone at her ear. "Hey babe," she sang in a lovey voice.

Jessa looked over to Jasmine and smiled. Jessa hoped whatever was going through Meesha's mind was only a case of pre-wedding jitters. It had to be since she knew how much her friend loved Connor and how much he loved her. Jessa hoped to one day have her own Connor. The man who would make her feel loved and appreciated.

Jessa and Jasmine continued to go through the clothes on the bed while they waited for the friend to get off her call.

By 11 p.m., Meesha was still on the phone. Jessa got restless waiting on the lovers' call to end. Jessa wished she had the ability to reach into the phone to pound Connor's head. Connor called Meesha about five times during the day since they arrived in Vegas. Their calls went on for hours. *Can't they stay away or refrain from talking to each other for more than five hours at a time? What was the point of the Bachelorette weekend, if Meesha spent most of the time on the phone?*

Jessa rolled her eyes when she heard giggling coming from Meesha's direction. She went into the washroom and got dressed in a short, black, spandex dress. When she was satisfied with her makeup, she stepped back into the bedroom.

"Come on Meesha; get off the phone already. It is getting late!"

Meesha mouthed something to Jessa and turned her attention back to the phone. Jessa seethed. Jasmine had left almost an hour ago to observe interactions between people. She was an author by profession and studied ways to improve her writing and the characters in her romance novels. She had a few bestsellers, with another on the way.

"I'm leaving. Call me when or if you get off the phone." After grabbing her purse and applying some of her perfume, she had left.

Jessa paused outside the suite's door and weighed her options. They had made plans to have fun, but now Meesha didn't seem interested. Staying in the suite was out of the question. She grabbed her phone from her purse and called Jasmine but to no avail. Trying to find Jasmine on the strip would be a worse option than remaining in the suite. She decided to head down to the hotel bar and just wait on her friends there since it was their original destination.

She felt her anger dissipating as she got out of the elevator and walked toward the bar. She could never be angry with her girls for too long. Besides, they'd had a good dose of fun, partying and touring Vegas since their arrival on Thursday evening. Today, Sunday, was their last night here.

She was positive a drink or two would get her in the right frame of mind for when her renegade girlfriends eventually joined her.

At the bar, Jessa hopped on a bar stool and ordered her first drink, tequila on the rocks with lime. She twirled her drink in her hand and sipped, savoring the smooth taste. She allowed her eyes to roam her surroundings. The first thing her eyes made contact with was the back of a familiar head: *Jaxon Jamison*.

Her mood darkened and her heart lurched as it always did whenever she saw or was near him. He was her brother's best friend and her own worst enemy. Jessa did not dislike anyone as much as she did Jaxon. He was cocky and annoying. He had tormented her life as a teenager with his relentless teasing.

He turned in her direction and his hazel eyes locked with her brown ones for a brief time. Realization dawned and then he grinned.

He got off his chair and sauntered in her direction. He was tall. She guessed he measured ten inches more than her own five foot five inches. His legs were long and his shoulders broad. He wore a dark suit. His thick brown hair was cut in a fade. He was all man and muscle. Her eyes appreciated the view.

When he got close enough to her, he said, "JJ." His voice was low, deep, masculine. He sounded more American than Canadian. His cologne washed over her and her stomach did a somersault. He was the only one who called her, *JJ*. Nowadays she didn't bother with correcting how he referred to her; he was never going to listen to her.

"Jaxon." She hoped her voice sounded as cold as she felt toward him.

"Are you here all by yourself?" he asked.

"None of your business," she replied, eager to dismiss him. She noticed the enigmatic quirk of his lips. He had always found her anger amusing and it had always angered her more.

"I will join you then," he declared and winked as he dragged a stool closer to hers. He removed his blazer and set it on the back on the stool before folding up the sleeves of his blue button down shirt. "I am waiting on Antonio, but he hasn't shown up," he let out even though she hadn't asked him.

Antonio was her brother's other best friend. Together, they owned a tech company worth millions, so she wasn't at all surprised at Antonio being in the vicinity.

He sat so close to her. The heat radiating from his muscular body wrapped itself around her. He looked more casual with the sleeves of his shirt folded. He tilted his head to face her and rubbed his eyes. She looked him over. His straight arrogant nose sat above a light moustache. His thick lips were devoid of a smile or grin. Upon closer observation, his skin appeared pale, paler than it normally was and there were shadows beneath his eyes, though they danced with amusement. She decided that he must be tired.

"Enjoy," she said and then got up to leave.

"Hey, hold on," Jaxon said, reaching out a hand to halt her departure. His touch sent signals coursing through her veins. Her knees felt somewhat weak. She felt her defenses slowly melting down. She looked at his offending arm across her waist, ignoring the tingling sensation she felt from his touch.

"Get your hands off me this instant."

"No." There was a cocky smirk on Jaxon's face. Jessa wanted to wipe it off with a slap.

She tried to maneuver out of his hold but he tightened his arm around her. Compared to Jaxon's strength, hers was nothing. She gave up easily.

"Sit," he commanded and when she arched a perfect brow in his direction, he added, "Can you please sit? I won't bite, unless you ask me to. I promise." He winked

Is he flirting with me? That couldn't be possible.

She wondered if she was hallucinating. He smiled again, exposing perfectly straight and white teeth and her knees almost buckled. It wasn't his normal egoistic smirk; rather it was a simple smile that didn't reach the eyes. She made no move to sit and neither did she try to get away from him.

His grip on her arm loosened and Jessa let out a relieved sigh. On one hand, she wanted to get away from him but on the other hand, her friends were still a no show and she did not want to leave the bar so soon. Her glass was still filled, barely touched. She weighed her options once more in her head, even though she already knew what she would do.

"You're a sight for sore and tired eyes, though."

Did Jaxon just compliment me?

"I can't say the same for you, Jaxon. You look like hell," she replied, wanting to bring out the side of him she knew and was comfortable with. Jerk Jaxon. She failed.

"I've been in meetings since the night before and I'm only now returning to the hotel." He wiped his face with his palm.

"That's your default state, Satan." Jessa smirked. She was still standing there even though his strong muscular arm no longer encircled her tiny waist.

Jaxon ignored her remarks and continued to look her over. "Sit, finish your drink."

She wanted to sit, however, she didn't want to be taking orders from him.

She would stand until she was ready to sit. Her chin tilted upward.

Seconds later, she felt powerful arms lift her onto her stool. Jaxon winked at her as she shot daggers at him with her eyes. She decided to not reprimand him for his actions, just this once.

Jaxon called out to the bartender with a wave of his hands exposing the beautiful gold watch strapped on his wrist. "Another drink for the lady and a scotch for me please, neat," he dished out his instructions. The bartender nodded and went about his duties.

"Jaxon, I do not remember telling you to get me another drink?" She narrowed her eyes at him and crossed her arms.

"You won't cut me any slack, will you?" Jaxon asked. He was still smirking.

"Nope," Jessa retorted.

"How about we try to be civil to each other Jessa, just for tonight. What do you say? Just two old friends at a bar having a drink. Yeah?" Jaxon asked.

"We're not old friends. Never have been, never will be." She took a sip of the tequila she had almost forgotten.

"Okay, fine. Well we can be two people at the bar who know of each other."

Jessa thought about it. It was surprising that she wasn't as bothered as she thought she might have been. It didn't help that Jaxon looked good enough to eat. *She would never admit that out loud.* She loved the attention she was getting from all the ladies who couldn't keep their eyes off him.

His biceps strained against the fabric of his shirt with every move. Her eyes drank in his confident movements. She had nothing else to do. The girls were God knows where.

"Okay," she agreed finally, taking a deep calming breath with her eyes closing for a second.

It took her some time to warm up to his kindness toward her but before the next hour was up, they did a few shots together while talking about mundane things.

"Let's play, 'never have I ever,'" Jessa suggested. She did not wait for a response from him. "I'll get the statements from online and read them out. If you've done whatever is read, then you take a shot." She searched her bag frantically for her phone, but each time her hands coiled around the cold metal object, she'd let it slip. She was already tipsy. After much effort, she pulled out her phone like it was some item she won at a contest.

"Game on," Jaxon responded.

Jessa clicked away on her phone and pulled up the statements from the, 'never have I ever', game.

"Never have I ever gone streaking," she read out loud.

Jaxon laughed and took a drink.

Jessa's mouth hung open. "You need to tell me about that."

He nodded, laughing lightly at her and told her that he would another time. For now, he wanted to win this game.

"Never have I ever had a one night stand."

Jaxon grinned then took a drink. Jessa stuck her tongue out at him and took a drink as well.

"You?" Jaxon said, utterly shocked. His lips tightened into a grim line.

"Yes me; it happened –"

Before she could continue, he held up his hand cutting her off. "Spare me the details, JJ."

She shrugged and continued the game. "Never have I ever slept with someone twice my age."

"If I didn't know any better, I would say that you're choosing statements directed at me."

Jessa giggled. "No I'm not. Drink up." She was.

He took a drink.

For the next half hour, Jessa completely lost herself in the game. As the game went on and more statements were read, Jessa and Jaxon continued to drink and laugh with each other to the point of intoxication. Several times throughout the evening, his eyes would flicker down to her lips, though she was unaware.

"Never.. Have I ever, have I married.. In Vegas."

After the last statement was read, they looked at each other and burst into a boisterous laughter.

"We have... one shot left... each and that ...was the last statement. Who won?" Jaxon asked.

"I don't.. know. Maybe we can rectify the last statement. Can't … we both.. win, be winners?" Jessa slurred.

* * *

Jessa slowly opened her eyes, then drew her palm across her forehead to quell the drum roll going on in her head. Her eyes surveyed her immediate surroundings. She suspected that the sun would soon saturate the room. Even without the light, she knew she had not slept in the suite she shared with the girls.

She gave herself a quick appraisal by running her palms down her body. She released the breath she had been holding when she felt her dress and her underwear in place. She felt a small movement next to her and froze. The movement stopped. Careful with her movements as to not make any noise or alert her unknown companion, she tilted her head in the direction of the movement. Her jaw became slack when she realized who was lying next to her.

Jaxon.

She guessed he was still asleep from his heavy breathing and the way his features were relaxed.

"Oh God," she groaned, covering her face with her palms.

Blurry images of the previous night began to play like a scene from a movie in her head. She couldn't remember it all but she knew she had done something stupid. She could recall some parts of the night, him leaning toward her, she too, leaning toward him. Their mouths coming in close contact but not sharing a kiss.

Not then.

Them holding hands and running off from the bar or was it the suite? She forced her brain to remember more. Had they just returned to the suite? Her head hurt more but she didn't stop trying to recall. She had to know what went down last night.

No. The last parts of her evening played in deliberate slow motion and she remembered the game, the statement about a Vegas marriage, him leaning in to her, them leaving the bar in search of a chapel. A chapel!

She felt it before she even verified with her eyes. Her mouth became dry as she raised her left hand and saw a simple plastic band nestled on her ring finger. Her eyes bulged at the sight and her breath held. She looked at Jaxon's bigger hand and saw an identical band on his ring finger.

She threw her hands over her mouth to keep from yelling out.

What have I done?

When her frantic heart calmed down a bit, she extracted herself from the bed making sure to not rouse Jaxon, grabbed her purse which was luckily on the floor of her side of the bed and then tip-toed out of the room as quiet as she could be.

Outside the room, her feet felt heavy and it took her some time before she felt ready to walk again. She paused, holding the wall for support as she tried to forget last night. Maybe if she tried to forget it, and acted like she couldn't remember, it would make the night less real. But she knew she was lying to herself. The night had happened and nothing she did would make it go away.

She realized that her suite was one floor down and decided to take the stairs. She traipsed along the stairs and held unto the banister for support. Her mind was still in disbelief.

Did I really do it? And with Jaxon, oh God. Maybe it wasn't legal.

She let her palm touch her forehead. A memory from the night before showed the Elvis impersonator explaining to them that the marriage would be legal and binding.

She remembered Meesha and Jasmine. She had never met them last night. She knew they would be worried sick about her. That was even worse than waking up beside Jaxon and finding out she was married.

She quickened her steps. Her need to get to their suite and reassure her friends that she was alright was great. Their suite was located at an angle and could be approached through three of the hallways on this floor. As she made the landing and advanced toward the suite, she noticed Jasmine and Meesha, walking toward their suite from the separate hallways. Jasmine still wore the dress from the night before. Meesha no longer wore the robe she had on last

9

night; instead, she wore a pink silk blouse and a pair of white jean pants.

At first Jessa thought they must have been out looking for her but when she got closer to them, they averted their eyes and looked down. No one spoke including her. Meesha fumbled for the electronic key in her purse, opened the door and they all walked in, still quiet.

"What did you girls do last night?" Jessa asked to break the silence.

Both girls turned toward her and answered at the same time. "I don't want to talk about it."

"Let's forget last night ever happened," Jasmine suggested as she walked into their bathroom. The others nodded in agreement. The shower came on soon after and it was only the sound of running water splashing against the tiled floor that filled the room.

Jessa closed her eyes for a second, trying desperately to erase the past eight hours from her mind. If only it was that possible.

Jaxon

nother phone call, another beep and her voicemail kicked in. *"Hi, this is Jessa, I can't get to the phone right now so please, leave a message."* Jaxon could not count the number of calls he had made to Jessa since Vegas. All his attempts to reach her had met dead ends. He could not forget what they did in Vegas. Nothing had happened sexually between them, he was sure of it. While he was drunk enough to consent to a marriage, he wasn't drunk enough to take advantage of her.

When he finally claimed her body, which he would, he wanted her to be sober. He wanted her to remember everything he did to her body vividly. He preferred for his conquests to be mentally present. Not that she was his conquest. She was his lawfully wedded wife. He had wanted her for years now, lurking in the shadows and watching her. Now that she was legally his, he didn't intend to let her go. It had been almost a month already, yet he still could not make contact with her. He was unable to turn her out of his mind.

When he had woken up in his suite alone on the morning of their wedding day, he wanted to get a flight back to Ontario immediately. His plans were thwarted when his business partner, Antonio, came into his suite and informed him about a meeting they could not miss in England. Business had taken him out of North America and kept him out throughout most of the month. He and Antonio wanted to expand their company to the European market and possibly open a branch there. He was mainly in charge of the development and manufacturing of technology portions of their company, while Antonio headed the video gaming development department. Their video games were very popular and profitable. They raked in millions every year.

He was finally back in Canada and his goal was to make contact with Jessa. They needed to have a conversation about their marriage. She had been deliberately ignoring his calls. If only she knew that she would not be able to get rid of him that easily. She had been his from the moment she responded to him in a biting remark after he had teased her about that Mohawk she had gotten on her seventeenth birthday. He was almost twenty-three years old at that time. Her quick tongue and sharp wit had captivated him. Her age at the time had cautioned him.

He was determined to make her his and he always got what he wanted. He could not and would not let Jessa slip out of his grasp. She was as beautiful as she was smart. She was employed as an elementary school teacher and she was the only woman to ever challenge him. He desperately wanted her and he could not simply let her slip out from his reach when everything between them seemed so permanent now.

Her physique was slender, not at all surprising since she did track and field. Her lips were full, made for kissing, made for kissing only him. They had kissed once that night and he wanted more. Her brown eyes were inquisitive. He had always liked Jessa, admired her even. Even though he teased her without mercy when she was younger, he had liked her. She never backed down from him. She always had a scathing reply in response to his. He hoped that the way he treated her in the past didn't hurt his chances now.

He needed to make amends with her. He would be careful with his approach and remind Jessa that they were legally bound to each other. He hadn't forgotten, and he would not let her forget. He threw on some casual clothes, a neck-scarf and penny loafers. He drove out to Kamal's. His plan was deceitful, but he needed to gather any information he could from Jessa's brother.

The drive to Kamal's apartment from his condo took about fifteen minutes. He rang the doorbell and waited. When the door opened, it revealed a blond young woman. Jaxon stepped in, a wide knowing smile played at his lips.

Kamal always had a different woman at his residence. He greeted the woman, just as Kamal emerged from the bedroom barefooted and wearing a bathrobe.

"Jaxxooon!" He called in his deep baritone.

"K Man!"

They shook hands and touched shoulders in greeting, their faces holding wide boyish grins.

"You have a guest," Jaxon stated the obvious.

"Marianne was just leaving," he replied, then turned to look at her. The young lady who had opened the door ambled toward the bedroom. A short while later, she reemerged with a purse and said a curt goodbye to Kamal before stepping out of the house.

"She doesn't seem very happy about leaving," Jaxon quipped.

Kamal waved the comment off with his fingers and Jaxon burst into a fit of laughter. "K man! One day, you will meet what you are hiding from on your doorstep."

"How will it get there?" Kamal laughed and then shrugged. He stepped behind the bar and fixed Jaxon a drink. He did not have to ask Jaxon what drink he wanted since his choice was always a scotch, neat. Jaxon walked toward the pool table.

Soon, they both had snooker sticks in their hands, knocking balls into pockets and laughing away. Jaxon was subtle when he asked his questions. He didn't want to alert Kamal to his real intentions.

"I saw your sister and her girls in Vegas," he said.

"Yeah, they were there for Meesha's bachelorette." Kamal struck a pose and shot at the balls, but he wasn't very successful and he hit his snooker stick on the floor.

"JJ pretended like she didn't know who I was," he said then chuckled. It was his turn to shoot at the balls.

"Are you surprised man? You two are like cats and dogs. My sister accepts zero bullshit."

"Are you calling me bullshit?" He turned to face his friend.

"If the cap fits, brother." They both laughed.

"She still teaches at the elementary school?" By now, they both had forgotten

13

about the game.

"Yeah, she may be vice principal soon," Kamal responded.

He asked a few more questions. He was like a hunter, threading through a field of dry leaves and twigs with extreme circumspection while Kamal responded, unsuspecting.

Jessa

*D*own on Joyceville Road, Jessa and Meesha sat with champagne glasses in their hands while a third glass sat on the small coffee table before them. Jasmine was trying on her third dress now. The first two had gotten thumbs down from her friends. One had made her look like her shape was missing and the other one had just been worse.

Meesha wanted to finalize the bridesmaids' dresses since her two friends disagreed on almost every dress she had chosen. The dresses were either too short, or too long or too revealing. Meesha decided that they each could choose their own style as long as the color was the same. Jessa's dress was chosen as soon as they got to the shop. It was a floor length, strapless chiffon dress. There was a really long split on one side. Meesha's bridal dress had been bought a month after the engagement.

Jasmine emerged from the dressing room wearing a dress that had Jessa laughing at the top of her voice. Meesha joined the laughter when she saw what Jasmine was wearing. Jasmine could not help but join the laughter, and then picked up her glass of champagne from the table.

"Are you guys gonna give advice instead of laughing?" She whined then took a large gulp of her drink.

"Sorry Baby but who made that?" Jessa asked. Meesha looked around the small area where they were. Jessa caught on to Meesha's actions and her own eyes widened as she looked around. Thank God the owner of the boutique wasn't standing nearby. "Try on the other one, Jasmine."

"I don't have a choice." Her smile took up the spaces on her face and the girls smiled back.

When Jasmine emerged again, they both nodded in approval. The dress was blush and floor length, like Jessa's but there were lace trimmings around the bust area and it was a V-neck. The bottom of the dress was made with chiffon and flared at the waist. It looked absolutely stunning on her….

"What do you think?" Jasmine asked, twirling.

"I like this one best," Meesha said. "It looks like it was made solely for you." Her approval was the only one needed since it was her wedding.

Jasmine looked at herself through the full length mirror and agreed. "Me too." She brushed her hands over her stomach.

Jessa walked up to Jasmine and pulled on the back of the dress.

"Ouch," Jasmine cried out in pain and then placed her hands over her boobs.

"Did I hurt you? I'm sorry. I was just thinking that the dress may need some alterations to make it fit more snugly on the top."

"My breasts just feel a bit tender," Jasmine said then blushed.

"You're probably PMSing, girl. It happens to me all the time," Meesha chirped in.

Jessa's hand was still on her friend's and she sensed when Jasmine froze. Her gaze switched to her friend's face and she saw her throat constrict and her wrinkled brow. Jasmine's brown hand traveled to her stomach then her light brown eyes blinked.

"Hey girl, are you okay?" Jessa asked, concern evident in her voice.

Jasmine cleared her throat and put on a tight smile. The smile didn't quite reach her eyes. "I'm good. Let's see about buying this dress."

Both Jessa and Jasmine sat next to Meesha while they waited for the shopkeeper to return. While they waited, they discussed the wedding and any other finalizations that were to be made. Jasmine remained quiet, which was strange. She wasn't the most talkative person but she held her own in a conversation.

"Where is the shopkeeper? It's been a while and I want to get out of this dress," whined Jasmine.

"She's probably with another client. Let's give her five more minutes and if she does not return, we will go find her," quipped Meesha. Her phone beeped, she looked down at it and a worried frown creased her brow. She turned off the phone, placed it in her purse, then faced her friends. "Besides, there's something I've been wanting to talk to you girls about. My heart's been filled with guilt since Vegas." Her fingers trailed along the rim of her champagne glass.

Jessa looked down at her hands to avoid making eye contact with either of her friends. What could Meesha have done that was worse than what she did? "You didn't do something stupid like get married to another man in Vegas, did you?" Jessa asked half-jokingly as she looked at her friend.

Meesha's head went backwards as if she had been slapped. "What? Of Course not!"

"Well you did say you felt guilty, and that was the only thing I could come up with that would you feel that way."

"Getting married in Vegas is tacky. I could never," responded Meesha.

I feel you girl," Jasmine added.

Jessa looked down at her hands again. Her ring finger no longer held that plastic ring. She had removed it from her finger as soon as she had gotten to the suite. It was now stored in her kitchen drawer.

How would she ever confess to getting married in Vegas now? They called it tacky and she felt just as they did.

She would get the annulment process started immediately. It was a drunken mistake. She would never pick up a glass again. Maybe after the annulment, she could confess and they could all have a good laugh about her *tacky* action.

I have to confess!" Meesha blurted. They had always been able to tell each other their secrets. Jessa's mind was going a mile a minute again. Even though she saw her friend struggling, she didn't want to talk about Vegas.

She was curious to know how her friends spent their last night, but she was opposed to sharing her own secret.

"Come on, do we really have to talk about that night?" Jasmine asked before Jessa could voice her own unwillingness.

"I want to talk about it. I did something and it's been eating at me," replied

Meesha.

"Did you kill someone?" Jasmine asked.

"Of course not!"

"Then what happened in Vegas should stay in Vegas," Jessa suggested.

"I couldn't agree more. Let's not talk about it," Jasmine said.

Meesha frowned and slouched on the sofa. She sighed deeply, silently giving up.

"I'll go find the shopkeeper. I want to get out of this dress," Jasmine informed the others as she stood up from the sofa and walked out of the dressing room.

"My girls will look all glammed up for my wedding," Meesha said, her good mood restored. "I can't wait for you girls to get married."

A shadow flitted across Jessa's face. Jasmine reentered the dressing room and told them that the shopkeeper would be with them in five minutes. Jasmine went to stand in front of the mirror and Jessa observed as she touched her breasts and turned and regarded herself at every angle in the mirror.

"I will be the matron of honor to whoever gets married next," said Meesha. Jessa's secret weighed her down.

Maybe I should just tell them and get it over with.

She dismissed the thought. If it had been another man, she may have confessed but it was Jaxon. Her friends knew that even under her biting remarks to him and about him, she had a crush on him. She denied their claims but they were adamant in their belief. It was too embarrassing. There was only one thing to do.

Annulment.

It would be like the wedding never happened. For that to happen, she would need to contact Jaxon. He was the one person in the world that she did not want to see and she had been ignoring his calls for almost a month now.

"Are you okay, Jessa?" It was Meesha. Her observations skills were on par with the RCMP's.

"Yes, yeah, I'm alright," she lied. The fog of her previous thoughts cleared and she looked into Meesha's concerned face. "I.. err.. I have to go," Jessa said, standing up.

"What? Why?"

"I have to go. There's something I need to do, for the school." She scrambled for her bag.

"Your school? It's Friday evening," Jasmine said.

"Yes, well there are some last minute things I need to handle for Monday's class," Jessa said.

Her friends' eyes bored into her skin and she feared they'd know she was lying.

"I need to go," she said and grabbed her bag from the seat. "I'll see you girls next week."

She almost stumbled to the ground on her way out, but maintained her balance. Outside, her car beeped and unlocked. She dived in, thankful for the reprieve from her friends. She hated lying to them and keeping secrets in general.

Why did she agree to have drinks with Jaxon? If she had sent him on his way, she wouldn't be in this mess now.

She started her car and went on her way. She went through the radio channels, till she stopped on the one for old school country music.

There will be significant snowfall in... The radio announcer began over the air.

Snowfall. *Trust Canada for always delivering on that end.* Jessa hated when it snowed. It made her sluggish and driving difficult. She stopped at the red traffic light. In a car beside hers, a couple kissed. She looked at the couple even after the traffic light turned green. The driver behind her honked multiple times and she was brought back to the present.

She remembered the feel of Jaxon's warm hands when he touched her, it sent shockwaves through her system. They had held hands, hugged, and laughed that night. They first kiss happened after the minister said, you may kiss the bride. It was short and chaste. They were too busy laughing to do much more. Everything from that night came back to her now. Her nerve endings had come alive by his gentle caresses against her skin. The more she thought of it, the more her body longed for him.

She hated her body's responses to him. Betrayal.

Her phone buzzed and she was grateful for the intrusion. However, it was

Jaxon again. Frowning, she looked away from the phone and faced the road. The man would not leave her alone. The thought of blocking his number held much appeal, but she wouldn't block him, at least not yet. She needed him.

By the time she pulled the car into the parking lot of the grocery store, some snow had begun to fall. She killed the engine and grabbed her scarf from the back seat, got out of the car and walked toward the entrance. She needed to restock so she grabbed a large trolley. Her fridge and cupboards were empty.

The store wasn't busy and she was grateful for that. Jessa walked down the aisles picking up the things she would need. She was in the cereal aisle trying to decide which ones to get when she heard someone come up behind her.

"Hey."

Jessa turned. It was one of the attendants. He was about her height, with blond hair and a crooked nose. There was something about his eyes that reminded her of Jaxon's. She sighed and shook her head. The more she tried to forget that night and him, the more thoughts plagued her mind.

"Do you need help?" The attendant asked with a slight smile.

"No, thanks for asking."

"Enjoy the rest of your evening."

The attendant turned and walked away and Jessa turned again to choose two boxes of cereal. There were just so many options, she did not know which to choose.

Her phone rang and she fumbled through the bag and fished it out.

"Hello," she said, breathlessly.

"Hello, Jessa, it's Gina Brown."

Gina was the principal at the school where she worked. She was not expecting any call from her.

"Hi Principal Brown, is everything okay?"

"Everything's fine. I only wanted to remind you to email your C.V. to me for the vice principal position. I'm supposed to submit it to the board on Monday."

The principal had informed her about the opening of the vice principal position right before she left for Las Vegas. Jessa knew she deserved it; she worked hard and even though some may consider her too young, she had ideas about moving the learning experience forward. In addition to that she was good with administrative work. As much as she loved her students, she wanted to move her career forward. With everything that happened in Vegas, she had completely forgotten about the offer.

"Are you still there?"

"Yes...I... uhm..." She took a deep breath. "I will send it to you as soon as I get home. Give me a couple of hours."

"I'll be waiting; enjoy the remainder of your evening." The line went dead. Jessa cursed. She picked up two random cereal boxes and left the aisle. She wondered how much work she would have to put in tonight on her C.V. which she last opened in three years ago when she applied for the teaching position.

It took her another thirty minutes to get everything she wanted from the store before she left. After leaving, she placed her purchases in the trunk of her car and peeled off. The snow was coming down heavier than it was earlier and the wind gusts were strong.

During her drive home, she made a mental note of all the things she would need to get done tonight. She needed to bring up all of her groceries, pack them in her fridge and cupboard, go over her C.V., and call her mother, who she hadn't spoken to in two days. That was unusual for them, since they normally spoke twice a day, but Jessa had been busy. She also needed to read up on the laws surrounding annulments.

What happens in Vegas, stays in Vegas. That was a lie she hoped would become true.

She pulled into the underground parking lot of the apartment building and killed the engine.

Jaxon

axon could not remember how long he had been waiting in front of the apartment building for his wife to finally get back. The doorman at the desk on the first floor of her condo building said she was not home. He had driven around for a while before returning.

A lot was going on in his mind. He decided if she was not here by ten pm, he would head home and come back in the morning. The snow was coming down heavily and his car felt like it was being pushed forward by the strong winds. He watched as an older looking man got out from the building and walked toward a car in the front parking lot. This was the third time the man did this since he'd begun waiting for Jessa.

He raised the heat inside his car. Since coming into town, he had checked into a hotel and then immediately came to Jessa's. While he now lived in Toronto, Jessa still lived in Kingston. Kingston was a small Canadian city, near Lake Ontario.

The headlights of a car blinded for a bit as it passed him and advanced toward the condo's underground parking. Even though visibility was low because of the snow, he recognized it instantly. It was Jessa's white Buick. He turned off his car and got out quickly. He hoped to slip under the garage door before it closed. He trudged through the snow quickly and made it just in time. He shook off the snow from his coat and hurried toward Jessa as she struggled with lifting grocery bags from the trunk.

"Let me help you with that," he said.

When she turned, disbelief flickered in her eyes. "Jaxon!"

While she stood frozen, staring at him, he grabbed the grocery bags from her trunk.

"You're stalking me now?" she asked, coolly. Her disbelieving eyes were now filled with loathe.

"Me? Never," he replied easily, ignoring her coolness.

"So what are you doing here?"

"Well I did try calling; however I think your phone probably doesn't work. I brought you a new phone, as well as to do a welfare check."

She rolled her eyes. Her brown skin appeared flushed and her small button nose looked swollen and light pink. He blamed that on the cold weather. She looked down at his preoccupied hands and made a move to grab her bags. He took a step back.

"Can you please hand me my bags? I'm perfectly capable of carrying them."

"I know you are, but I won't allow you to carry them while I'm here to do so."

She rolled her eyes again. She closed her trunk, grabbed her purse and computer bag from the back seat and then locked her car. She marched to the elevator without looking back.

He could not stop staring at her backside as he walked behind her. She was wearing black trousers and a mustard blazer.

So Mrs. Jamison, why have you been ignoring my calls?" he asked when they got into the elevator and she groaned in response.

"It's Miss Smith, and please let's not discuss this here."

"That's fair."

The rest of the elevator ride was done in silence. When they got to the fourth floor, they get out of the elevator and Jessa led the way to her apartment. When they got to her front door, she paused as though assessing what her next move would be. Jaxon's lips turned up at the corners at the thought of her coming up with a plan to get rid of him. Her shoulders slumped and she finally unlocked her door, giving up. She was only going to unlock her door for him, only let him into her house and nowhere else.

"Come in," she said sweetly. "The kitchen is that way." She pointed to the area where her kitchen was. "You can put the bags down in there."

Jessa locked her door after Jaxon entered and armed her security alarm. Jaxon came out of the kitchen minutes later and looked around her room. Just like her kitchen, her living area was modern with neutral colors. Her sectional sofa was white leather and there was a thick white rug in front of the sectional. There were pictures of children all over her walls and a huge television hung over a fireplace. Her place was cozy.

"You can have a seat while I put the groceries away. Please take off your boots before stepping unto my rug."

"Do you need any help?"

"No, things will move faster if I do it myself."

He shrugged off his coat, removed his boots and took a seat on her sofa. He had a feeling that she was trying to avoid having the conversation they needed to have. He wouldn't push her. He would move at her pace. For now.

About fifteen minutes later, she came into the living area and sat on the other end of the sofa. Jaxon watched her, his eyes taking in every gesture she made. Her braids were now tied back at her nape. She looked beautiful; she always did. He bet if he saw her after she was hit by a truck, she'd still make his heart skip beats. His eyes drifted to her lips, but he looked away.

"Ready to talk?" he asked.

"Listen," she started and folded both of her legs underneath her on the sofa. "What we did was a stupid drunken mistake. We don't need to make it a bigger deal than it is. We can annul the marriage quickly and never speak of the incident again. We can then get on with our lives and marry people we actually love." Her voice was gentle and a relaxed smile played at her lips after announcing her plan.

He hated how gentle she was about an annulment. Suspicion crept into his thoughts and his eyebrow arched. "You're dating someone?" He had fully overlooked the fact that she may have a man in her life. He didn't care anyway. She was his wife, whether she liked it or not.

"That is none of your business!"

"I disagree. I'm your husband." He sounded much harsher than he had intended to.

"I said my piece. I don't plan to engage with you further!"

"We need to settle this. Come up with a more reasonable plan. Not an annulment."

"If not an annulment, then what? You can't really expect us to keep this marriage going? We don't even like each other."

Jaxon snorted. He liked her very much and he did intend on keeping the marriage. He had not expected her to immediately agree with keeping it, however. Her ignoring him for almost a month told him as much. He did expect her to hear him out though. They had always had something that bubbled below the surface even when they teased each other. Her reluctance would make winning her over more fun. "I like you."

He could tell she was taken aback by her slackened mouth and unsteady gaze. She finally regained herself and unfolded her legs from under her.

"Listen, I don't know what –"

He moved quickly toward where she sat and pressed his lips against hers. She froze but he continued to nibble on her closed lips. When he stuck out his tongue to probe her lips open, she gave no resistance. She opened her mouth and melted toward him. The kiss became deep, passionate. She gave him as much as he gave to her.

His hands trailed her shoulders and the sides of her breasts.

Jessa

essa breathed deeply and clung on to him. She had been waiting for this moment for a long time. His lips were soft and his breath warm. His lips. Was there anything, softer, sweeter? She thought not. She was lost in the frenzied kiss.

Her arms moved from between their bodies and hooked behind his neck. He continued to kiss her fiercely. His hand kneaded her breast and his thumb stroked her perky nipple. She moaned as shockwaves from his delicious onslaught moved through her body.

She was in heaven. She felt weightless as warmth surged through her core by his machinations. His hands felt strong and demanding on her breasts. She combed her fingertips through the short hairs at his nape. His hands were under her blouse now and the direct contact to him sent tingles down to her toes. Had she ever been so thoroughly aroused?

"I want you," he said breathlessly as he created a trail of kisses from her neck, down to her shoulders. She felt elated at the thought of him wanting her as much as she wanted him.

He finally raised his head from her neck and looked into her eyes. Locked in an intense gaze, they were both unaware of the darkness surrounding them. Suddenly, she remembered that she should be hating him and stood, moving away from him quickly, like his touch had burnt her. Maybe his lips and fingers had caused a sensation that felt as hot as fire, but it was in a very good way. The fire he had caused was the best she had ever known.

"What happened to the lights?" She walked over to her light switch and flicked it a few times to no avail.

While she flickered the different slight switches in her home, she was vaguely aware of him striding to the large window.

"I think the power is out throughout the town, JJ. Power lines must be down. The snow has gotten worse as well. Come have a look."

He was right; the entire neighborhood looked gloomy and snowy. She could also hear the strong winds. She hoped her windows would survive the wind. Only in Canada would there be a snowstorm in the middle of April. Just last week, she had packed away her winter clothes and eagerly moved all her spring and summer outfits to the forefront of her closet.

She groaned. "I hate winter."

"Well that's too bad then. I was about to ask you to help me build a snowman." She looked up at him and saw the twinkle in his eyes and the smile that played at his lips.

She couldn't help smiling herself.

The moment was broken by the ringing of her phone. She went in search of it. She grabbed it and returned to the window to stand next to Jaxon.

"Hey, girl." It was Jasmine on the other end.

"Hey," Jessa replied.

"Have you seen how terrible it is outside? I hope you got home already," Jasmine said.

"I did, thankfully."

"Glad to hear it. I wanted to know how you were doing as well. You left pretty quickly earlier."

Jessa pinched the bridge of her nose and for the next ten minutes, she assured her friend that she was okay. They discussed the current storm and Jasmine informed her that roads would be closed since several trees and poles had fallen. They went over details of Meesha's upcoming wedding and she informed Jasmine about her plans to apply for the vice principal position at her school. Her friend was happy for her. The call finally ended when Jasmine mentioned preparing dinner.

She turned away from the window with the intention of apologizing to Jaxon but found the apartment empty after a search. Her heart skipped a bit. He had probably left, no doubt hoping to get back to wherever he was staying. She refused to explore the feeling of disappointment she felt as his leaving and hoped instead that he made it to his destination safely in this weather.

Resigned, she walked toward the sofa and flopped down on it. She felt like she should probably light a few of the candles she purchased from the body store but she didn't feel like it yet. Besides it wasn't pitch black; she could still see the shapes of different furniture. She could also still feel the tingles from Jaxon's kiss and his touch. He had said earlier that he didn't want an annulment; what did that mean for them? Did he want a divorce instead? But that didn't make sense because he had also told her he liked her. Was he teasing her again? If he was, it would be very cruel of him.

Her front door was pushed open and a snow covered Jaxon stood at the threshold. He shook off the show, stepped it and closed the door behind him. Jaxon stared into the dark room and Jessa jumped up from where she sat. He didn't leave after all. She would ignore the warmth spreading throughout her chest by his return. She dreaded spending the night alone with the storm going on outside.

"My car is covered in snow and a tree fell on it. I don't think I can move it tonight."

"That sucks. What do you plan to do?"

He grinned and raised his right hand. She saw the gym bag then.

"You stuck with me for tonight."

"Oh." She couldn't bring herself to say anything else. Wanting him to stay with her and having him actually spend the night filled her with dread. It suddenly felt too intimate.

"I could try walking back to my hotel."

She gasped and her eyes went wide.

"You can't possibly! You will freeze to death for sure."

He chuckled. She realized that he was just pulling her leg.

"It's a comfort to know that you care about my welfare." He dropped his gym bag near the door.

"I don't. I just don't want to become a widow before I have a chance to end this marriage," she bit out.

"So you acknowledge that you're my wife?"

"My goodness you are so full of yourself."

"Sure, tell yourself whatever you want to feel better."

He smiled and she wanted to smack the smile from his luscious lips.

"Where is your washroom? I wanna grab a shower before the water turns cold."

"It's right down the hallway on your left. Save some hot water for me. I'll go find the candles," she said.

Jaxon

∾

Jaxon laid face up on Jessa's pull out sofa bed. After he had showered earlier she had made it clear that he would be sleeping on the couch. Her second bedroom was being used as her home office. He didn't mind though; at least they were under the same roof and he had some access to her. He knew that he would need to call a town truck in the morning for his car. It was damaged severely and he doubted very much that it would be of use to him again. The tree fell across his car and caused a huge dent between the driver's seat and those in the back. His windows and windshield were also busted.

Earlier, she had fixed them a small supper using Kraft dinner. He was thankful that her stove wasn't electric; if it was, then they may have starved. While they ate, they barely spoke to each other. She had placed candles in the kitchen and the living room and placed some of the milk and the meat that she bought earlier in the snow on her balcony to preserve it.

His mind could not stop picturing them lying on her bed, naked. He knew it was only a matter of time. The sexual tension between them was at a boiling point and it would soon combust. Jessa was still fighting against it. He could see it in her brown eyes during dinner. She avoided looking at him and avoided touching him.

He thought of his old man and wondered how he was doing. He hadn't seen or spoken to his dad in over a year. The relationship had been estranged long before that. When his mom passed away, his dad became more withdrawn. He became a different man than the nurturing father Jaxon was used to. His mom died when he was eleven from cancer and he lost both of his parents on that day. His dad became a shell of a man, more introverted. Jaxon, being the only child of his parents, had to go through it alone. He missed his mother and hoped that she was proud of him. He knew she wouldn't be pleased with the relationship between her husband and only son.

Even though his dad never reached out, Jaxon decided that he would try calling him in the morning. He wanted to ensure that he was doing okay. If he was being honest, he missed him. The dad he had before cancer took his mom. The man who he called dad now was in a constant state of melancholy and he never stayed more than three minutes on the phone with his only child.

His phone beeped and it illuminated the room. He reached for it.

It was Lysa; they had slept together a few times and gone out on a few dates. He had broken things off with her after he got married, before he left Vegas. He had done it over the phone since it couldn't be helped. She wasn't giving up though. She texted him every day and told him how much she missed him. He was becoming annoyed.

He deleted the message without even reading it. He had no interest in her whatsoever. He had told his business partners earlier that he was taking a few days off. They didn't know why though and he hoped after spending more time with Jessa they would learn the reason. He was worried about Kamal's reaction to finding out he married his sister. Her entire family may just flail him. That was a risk he was willing to undertake though.

He curled into himself as the cold started seeping in through the walls. Having no electricity meant there wasn't any heat. He imagined Jessa in her bed alone and wondered if she was cold. Did she yearn for his warmth the way he yearned for hers? Jaxon fell asleep with thoughts of Jessa. Her smile, her body, her comebacks; she was his wife and tattooed in his mind.

The next morning, Jaxon's eyes sprang open. He had been having a nightmare involving his mother, but when he finally woke, he could not remember anything about it. The only thing that pointed at the nightmare was the way his chest heaved up and down.

Disoriented, he could not recognize where he was. The set up was different from his home, and the furniture was scantier than his own. It wasn't a hotel either; at least not a hotel where he would willingly spend the night.

He sat up from whatever it was he was lying on and tried getting his mind to focus. The day was just breaking. His Cartier watch said it was 6:15 in the morning, an hour later than he usually woke up. A picture of JJ's smiling face hung on the wall and he remembered where he was and everything that happened last night.

He stood up, stretched and walked to the large window. The snow was still coming down heavily. The entire street was covered in snow. The cars parked on the streets were also invisible under the snow.

He turned back toward the room and wondered if JJ was still asleep. He walked to the kitchen and after a quick search in the fridge he decided to prepare breakfast. He gathered his ingredients and went on to work quickly and efficiently in making them breakfast. He placed a medium sized pan which was filled with water to make coffee on the stove, and then set the small dining table.

As if she sensed breakfast was done, Jessa walked into the kitchen. He went over to her side and placed a kiss on her forehead.

Jessa

To say she was surprised by what greeted her in her kitchen was an understatement. Jaxon moved around her small kitchen with ease. The aroma coming from his meal caused her stomach to growl silently. He raised his head and spotted her. A half smile took over his lips and he walked over to where she stood and kissed her forehead.

"Good morning," he said sweetly. "Slept well?"

"I did," Jessa lied. She was up more than half of the night thinking of the man sleeping in her living room. She wished things were different between them. Wished she could march to her living room and demand that he join her in bed. When she realized that she wouldn't get him off of her mind easily, she had pulled out her phone and opened the cloud to go over her C.V. She then fixed it and emailed it to her boss.

"You made breakfast?" she stated, more than asked.

"Come, let's eat," he said. He pulled out a chair for her and she sat before he moved away to claim the chair opposite the one she occupied.

She took reluctant bites from her eggs and toast and was pleasantly surprised. They weren't oily or salty. "The bread is just the way I love it. Not so crunchy, yet not so soft."

"I know," Jaxon said smiling.

She took a sip of her coffee and it washed away some of the resentment she had towards him. Some, not all.

"How did you learn to cook?" she asked.

"I dated a chef."

"Interesting." She took another bite of her meal, stabbing the eggs.

"Leanna; that was her name. She taught me how to prepare gourmet meals. You should see what I can do with meat. I make a mean roast beef."

"She taught you well then."

A vine of envy traveled from her toes up to her face. She was sure she was green now. She didn't understand the negative emotion. It wasn't as if she and Jaxon were a real couple.

"She did," Jaxon continued.

"How come it didn't work out between you two? You could have married her."

He laughed and said, "And miss this lovely breakfast with you?"

"Stop playing and tell me."

His grin turned into a slight smile. "I had my eyes and heart set on someone else."

He watched her intently and heat crackled between them. She thought she would melt for sure with all the emotions running through her. She wondered about the woman who held his heart and why there was a surge of jealousy running through her. She wouldn't explore that emotion.

Now he was stuck with her and not the woman he loved.

"Do you still have your heart set on that other woman?" She knew she was probing but she needed to know about the one who had captured his heart.

"I do," he said simply and stood up to bring the empty plates to the sink. She suspected that he wouldn't open up any more about this woman so she decided to bring the conversation back to a mutual subject.

"Jaxon," she called, "have you told anyone about our... the marriage?"

Since this faux pas in Vegas, she struggled with saying the word *marriage*. How could a twenty-four year old elementary school teacher allow herself to be in this predicament? She was responsible. She paid her bills on time, never used bad words and called her mom every day. This marriage was the second most stupid thing she'd ever done in her life. The first was the giant tattoo on her lower back.

"I haven't and I won't unless you want me to," Jaxon said.

Jessa sighed, releasing the breath she didn't know she was holding. "You have to admit, it's a little embarrassing." She chuckled.

"I'm not embarrassed," he stated.

"Come on, Jaxon. Don't start. You know it was a drunken mistake. Neither of us meant to be married to each other."

"Right," Jaxon said as he collected her empty plates from the table and placed them in the sink. When he turned back to her, his face was stony. "I'll use your bathroom now."

"Go ahead," she replied.

She watched his retreating back. She wasn't intentionally being spiteful. She didn't understand the change in his mood. She was right in saying the marriage wasn't planned. It wasn't going to work. He could have more luck with the woman that stole his heart.

She didn't want them to have any more animosity between them and felt a bit guilty. But these things needed to be said. He had to know that the two of them were miles apart in thinking. They were not meant to be married.

She went to her sink and finished on the dishes he left half attended to.

With the dishes done, she headed to her room. She needed to create a lesson plan for her students. The folder with her activities was on the bedside table in her room. The door was partly open and she walked in. Jaxon stood, in all his naked glory, before her mirror.

She held unto the door post as she took him in with her eyes. His skin was a bit tanned and his biceps huge. His back was large and ripped. Long strong legs extended from a firm ass. What would it feel like to wrap her legs around his waist? Her mouth went dry.

She did not know how long she stood there drinking in his sheer masculinity before Jaxon turned toward the door. She wanted to turn away from his gorgeousness, but her eyes trailed down his body until her eyes made contact with the temple that had formed beneath his boxers.

She tilted her head slightly and bit her bottom lip as her mind thought of the million things she could do with him. Her eyes sought his and the corners of his lips twitched.

She swallowed and quickly turned away from him. The folder she needed was lying on the table near her queen size canopy bed. She scurried to the table, grabbed the folder and headed out of the room with dignity she didn't feel.

She did not want Jaxon to know that he had rattled her, that the thought of what it would feel to have their bodies locked in an intimate embrace was starting to mess with her mind.

But he had *rattled you.*

She forced the little voice in her head to keep quiet. She was out of the room. She dashed to her office and slammed the door shut. She locked the door and pressed her back against it, hoping it would keep everything she just saw out of her mind. It didn't work.

What sort of man was Jaxon? What was he doing staring at that gorgeously crafted body in the mirror? What was his problem? Did he sense her arousal? How can one man be blessed as impressively as Jaxon? A shiver ran through her heated body. Every other man she had seen naked, paled in comparison to him.

Jessa realized she was breathing too hard. The more Jaxon stayed here, the more her defenses against him crumbled. The weather was still bad outside and the roads were still blocked. She hoped they roads would be cleared soon, she didn't know how long she could last before giving in to her body's urgings. She wanted Jaxon gone and the power restored.

Jessa's hands slowly slid down her nightdress. She whimpered when her fingers made contact with her taut nipples. She imagined Jaxon's lips on them, his tongue circling the buds. His eyes taunting and arousing her as he did so.

She could almost see his head, buried in her chest, she could almost feel him too. Her fingers trailed down her body and she visualized Jaxon's lips sweeping her body instead. There was only her and Jaxon in the room because they were the only two who mattered. She imagined Jaxon taking what he wanted and giving her everything she needed.

She clamped her thighs together, trying to keep the heat from building up down there. She was at no luck. She finally allowed her fingers to make contact with where she wanted to feel him most. The action overwhelmed her.

She closed her eyes and released a sound of ecstasy as her fingers continued to rub on her clit.

Her feet wobbled like jelly. She didn't stop imagining all the bad, good, things he could do to get if she let him and her finger movements intensified. She used her free hand to cover her mouth as her moans of pleasure intensified.

Jaxon

axon stood in the room alone, naked, after Jessa had left. It didn't surprise him when he turned and saw JJ standing there, ogling at his naked body. He knew she had been there for a while. He knew she was pleased with what she saw. Most girls were. All he wanted was to pin her below him and possess her.

His desire for her was primitive and savage. He pushed it away, but he could not stop thinking about the way her hips swayed in that transparent nightgown. It was excruciating to look and not be able to touch. He wanted to confine her to this room and drag her to bed. It took everything in him to stand there and not react.

He would wait for her to come to him. He suspected their time would come sooner rather than later. That was the good thing that came out of this storm. They were stuck here together and it caused whatever spark of attraction they had between them to bloom further.

Tired of the wrestling going on in his mind, he got dressed quickly and strolled out of the bedroom. He needed to find something to keep his mind occupied. Any more thoughts on her body would send him in search of her to claim her. That was the last thing he wanted. He wanted her to let her guard down and seek him out.

He walked past the kitchen and there was no sign of JJ. He assumed that she was still in her home office. He had heard the door slamming earlier. He put on his coat, boots and a tuque. He stepped out of her apartment and walked the small distance to the elevator. Thankfully it was on her floor already and unoccupied. He took it down to the ground floor and found himself outside the condo complex in a matter of minutes. The snow came up to his thighs and he had to plod his way to where his car was parked.

His car was still covered in snow. Not that he'd expected the snow to magically disappear. The tree that had fallen onto his car could barely be seen under all of the snow.

"Damn," he muttered.

His biceps bulged as he tried to push the fallen tree away from his car. It was heavier than he thought and he realized it would take more than his strength to get it off. A man came out from the rolling door of the apartment building and walked toward him.

"Need a hand?" he man asked. He had red hair and a square jaw. He also had slits for eyes, but he had a ready smile on his lips. He looked to be in his mid-twenties. Jaxon was sure that he was older than the man.

"Sure," Jaxon replied.

The man joined him and they heaved together. The tree shifted an inch.

"I was watching you from my window. A pity that this tree destroyed such a sweet ride," the man said with a look of regret. Jaxon understood his remorse. This car was the latest Mercedes Benz model.

"Insurance will cover it. I'm just glad I wasn't in the car when it happened."

"I hear that."

The two men heaved at the tree again, and the thick stem shifted.

"The car will need a lot of repairs," the man continued.

"Yes," Jaxon replied. He was not really listening. He was not in the mood for small talk. He did not care about the car - he had four more and it was a shame this one got destroyed and would probably end up in junkyard. The damage seemed too excessive for repair. Then again, he was not a mechanic…

"Jeez, it's as cold as the devil's tits. It sure would be nice to be under some warm covers with a beautiful woman right now," the man let out as they heaved again.

"Hmm," Jaxon replied non-committedly. He did not need his mind straying back to the reason he was out here in the first place. Of course, he would prefer to be loving on JJ in her bed instead of doing this tedious task. He wished the other guy would shut up. But he had to be thankful that he was even helping him. If he had to listen to his rambling then he guessed it was a fair exchange.

"Winter storms can do that to a man. Make you wanna get warmth from a woman. You know, you strike me as a man that knows his way around women, so I'm going to ask you for a little advice."

Fuck, Jaxon cursed in his head. Didn't some people understand the concept of silence? What exactly did he want now? They hauled the tree for the last time and it rolled off the car, taking a rearview mirror with it. The roof was completely caved in.

"So this lady that lives in this building. I think she's single. I haven't seen any man around. She has this lovely brown complexion, like rich cocoa and the prettiest brown eyes a man can ever wish to look into every morning. I've been thinking of asking her out, you know? But she always seems to be busy. I think she's a teacher."

"What?" Jaxon's mind finally focused when he heard the tail end of the description. If he had heard correctly, the man just described JJ and he did so in a better way than he ever could, which made him envious of the young buck.

"What do you think? How do I start a conversation?" the man asked, arms akimbo.

"Don't."

"What? What do you mean?" His brows drew together in confusion.

"Is she about five feet five inches, slender, cute little ass?"

"Yes, that's her, the black girl. Her ass sure is cute."

"She's my wife," he responded through gritted teeth. He was slowly losing his patience.

"You don't say!"

"*I say*. She's my wife and therefore off limits."

"I did not know, man. I've never seen you around." He dusted his palm on the thigh of his faded blue jeans.

"It doesn't matter. I'm telling you that she is my wife and I don't share. I keep what's mine."

"Well you're a lucky sonovabitch, man. She's a keeper."

"I know, she's mine to keep." He didn't need someone telling him; he had known since forever.

The man walked away after apologizing again and saying his goodbyes. Jaxon was glad to be rid of him.

He pried his trunk open and pulled out a shovel. He dug out the snow around his car. It was silly and futile, seeing as the snow was still falling and his car would get towed, but he needed to do something aside from sitting idly in JJs home and imaging her naked in different positions. The cold seeped through his skin but he ignored it.

Something solid but soft struck his head as he bent to lift the shovel. It was cold. He turned and Jessa stood near the garage entrance of the complex giggling, but trying hard to not appear as if she was by covering her mouth with her gloved hands.

"No you didn't," he growled.

In response, she sent another snowball after him. This one made contact with his nose and spattered on his face. He wiped it off, threw the shovel into his car through the broken windshield and bent to make his own snowballs.

By the time he stood straight, his target was off in a sprint through the thick snow and had placed much distance between them. Jessa moved very fast. She dodged all of his projectiles and landed yet another one squarely on his head.

"Goddammit!" Jaxon howled, amusement mixed with determination on his face. He dodged one of Jessa's snowballs. But no matter how fast he moved or how well he hid, her other snowballs found their target.

Tired of being Jessa's prey, he took off running in her direction. Jessa caught on to his intent late, before she could react, he had already wrestled her to the ground. He laid his full weight on her body and stared down at her.

"Dammit, JJ," Jaxon said as another snowball hit his face. He pinned both of her hands between them to prevent another attack.

Jessa chortled; she looked nothing like the defiant woman he left in the apartment. She looked happy, just as she had in Vegas when they played that game. Seeing her like this did something to him. As if sensing the change in the atmosphere, her laughter subsided, and she licked her lips. She stared at his mouth.

"Your car is pretty messed up." If she thought to change the direction of his thoughts, it wouldn't work. He would claim those enticing lips.

"I don't care about the damn car."

He bent his head closer to hers and pressed his mouth against hers. Her lips were cold, unsurprising considering the weather conditions. Soon enough, her lips began to heat up under the leisure onslaught of his.

He loved kissing her; he loved having her in his arms. He loved the way her lips warmed up to his, welcoming him. He savored the moment before he drew back. Her eyes were closed. Her eyelashes fluttered as her brown orbs came into view again. It was too much for him. He claimed her lips again. His wife's lips, the ones he would never get enough of. It was a slow kiss that clearly told each how much they needed the other.

He did not know how long they lay in the snow in below freezing weather kissing each other. But when he started to feel his toes becoming numb in his boots, he reluctantly dislodged his lips from hers. He placed two more chaste kisses on her lips before opening his eyes and staring at her.

"How do you aim so well?" He asked.

"My brother tortured me with this game as a child. I had to learn or lose," she replied breathlessly. He followed her eyes - they were on his lips. She wanted that kiss again, and so did he. He leaned in and kissed her and once again, she welcomed him warmly.

Jessa

J essa frowned as she shook the dice. She stared at the snakes and ladders game keenly. She wanted a good number so she would not fall victim to a snake. Her eyes met with Jaxon's and she glared at him. He smirked in return. His peg was farther ahead than hers. Luck was never on her side when she played this game. She always got eaten up by the longest snake or the second longest one.

She blew on the dice, said a prayer and released them.

"Five," she said, twisting her lips.

When she moved her peg up, it landed in the mouth of a snake which sent her about 50 steps back.

"Oh dang it!" She cursed.

Jaxon roared with laughter. She wanted to turn the game over and stomp to her room.

Since coming back from outside yesterday evening, they'd played board games together. There was an unspoken truce between them and she liked it very much. She loved the easy kisses he imposed on her lips or cheeks or forehead, the lingering touches when he handed her something and his heated stare when he caught her smiling.

"I don't understand why you're laughing." She frowned. Jaxon's laughter became out of control after what she said. He tumbled back on her bed with glee.

"Will you roll the dice or not?" Jessa asked as she crossed her arms under her breasts.

Five minutes later, when his laughter was finally under control, he rolled the dice. Jessa clenched her teeth and wished him misfortune.

The very opposite happened. He got four and it brought him to the bottom of a ladder, which took him twenty places upward.

"No, dammit! This game is rigged against me. I can never win."

"The game is not rigged. I love this game," he said, chuckling.

"Look who's talking all of a sudden. I love how silent you were when we played Monopoly," Jessa said, smiling, throwing in the fact that he lost that game to her of course.

"You won only because you bought up most of the more expensive properties and won most of the money in free parking and from chance." His defense was lame to her.

"And I'd have kept beating you if you had not run away."

"I didn't run away."

But he had. Last night, he had been bubbling with energy and confident about being the *Monopoly king*. After making out in the snow the day before, he carried her to the elevator, where they had continued making out till an elderly woman joined them. They stopped kissing but didn't break their embrace. When they got to her apartment, he had made them a light supper. He was a much better cook than she was after all.

After eating, she had suggested they play board games in her room. She loved how she'd caught him staring at her. She loved the easy kisses he imposed on her lips, cheeks or forehead, the lingering touches when he handed her something. She was glad to have him here.

"You did run away," Jessa pressed further. "And with your tail tucked between your legs too."

"I'll show you what's tucked between my legs."

It was a threat but she was saved from having to reply from her ringing phone.

She picked up her phone from the side table and accepted the call.

"Jessa?" Her mother's voice came over the phone. It was laced with concern.

"Hi Mom, how are you?" She asked.

"I'm fine, just worried about you."

"Don't be. I'm alive as you can tell." She rose a finger in the air, excusing herself.

"Who are you giving this attitude to? You're not too old to get smacked in the butt."

"Mom, I wasn't giving an attitude." She rolled her eyes as a small smile crept up her face.

"Did you just roll your eyes at me?" Her mom knew her so well. She didn't respond to the question.

She and her mom continued to go back and forth. That was how their relationship went. Her mom always believed she was giving attitude, when she wasn't. Her mom got pleasure in reminding her that she was the one who gave birth to her and Jessa always reminded her mom of *once a man twice a child.* This was their unique bond and Jessa loved it.

They talked about other random stuff and she also told her mom about sending her application for the vice principal position with her school. Her mom was proud and boasted that she would get it since nobody else deserved it more than her daughter.

She did not tell her mom that Jaxon was stuck in her apartment with her or about the marriage. The marriage she wasn't so sure what she wanted to do about again.

"I just don't feel okay knowing you're up there all alone. If something happens to you, how will you get help?"

"Mom, nothing will happen to me. I have been through blizzards before. This one is no different. My fridge is stocked, though most of my meat and drinks are in the snow on the balcony to keep them fresh, since I have no power."

"I don't know. What if you fall and hit your head?" her mom continued stubbornly.

"Mother, I'm fine! If anything happens, I'll call you. The roads should be cleared soon."

That seemed to calm her mother down a bit. With her next words, the panic in them was toned down.

"When did you stock up?"

"Last Friday, after the dress fitting."

"You're sure you're fine?"

"I am. What about you Mom? Do you and Dad have enough food?"

"Girl you know I buy a month's worth of food. I'm good for another two weeks, three if need be."

"Good, tell Dad hey for me and tell him to not shovel any snow. It's not good for his back."

"You know how stubborn that man is. He's shoveling the walk path in front of the house now."

"Mom you need to hide the shovel from him."

"You know he'll just get another one."

Jessa sighed. Her mom was right. Her next words however tried to calm Jessa down.

"Don't worry about your dad. He is stronger than you think. You stay safe now, Baby Girl."

"I will. You too, Mom."

The phone line went dead and Jessa breathed in deeply. A conversation with her mum was always an hour and a half long affair. Growing up, she had been too small for her age and was always bullied. In fact, one of her tormentors back then was the man spending time in her house.

A man she was very attracted to. The way she felt about him frightened her. He would have the power to hurt her if she allowed herself to give in. She didn't want him evading her fragile sense of self-preservation, although she feared it may already be too late. Something smelled really good. Jaxon must have prepared dinner while she was on the phone. She had been too caught up in the call, so she didn't realize when he got up.

"Hey," Jaxon's voice came over her shoulder as his hands brushed against her sides. His warm breath washed over her skin and stroked the embers within her core.

She stiffened and moved away from him. She had been facing the window for who knows how long. She could not bring herself to turn back and look into his handsome face. This was a mistake. She should have asked him to leave the moment he had dropped off her groceries.

"Is everything alright?" he asked, concern etched in his words.

Jaxon seemed different from how he was before. Or was he always this reasonable and she the one who created the drama between them? He never insulted her in his teasing. It was more playful on his part. Had she misconstrued him all these years? She thought not; she couldn't have. She did not want to forget the past. Remembrance made her hold firm against his advances now.

"I'm okay. My mom called and she was worried about me."

She braced herself, turned and smiled at him. She was back in control, and had come up from the child that she had shrunk to just moments ago. She was now an adult, capable of hiding her thoughts.

"Did you tell her I was here?"

"Of course not! She would probably start planning a wedding. She loves you a lot you know and she *ships* us."

"I love your mom, she's a very smart woman. Nothing wrong with a second wedding either. Maybe we'll both be sober at this one."

"Jaxon…." she sighed.

"Come," he said, cutting off whatever she was about to say. He led her away from the window, holding her soft hands in his as he traced patterns with his thumb. She could have very well withdrawn her hand from his, but she didn't want to. She liked the tingling sensation that his hands brought. She loved the way hers fitted into his like they were made for each other.

They got to the kitchen and her mouth fell open as she did a double take. There were candles lit up all around the kitchen. It produced a soft glow that spoke of intimacy. Deep intimacy. Flower petals were scattered beautifully on the table. The sight was breathtakingly beautiful.

Jaxon smiled at her when she looked his way, lost for words.

"This is beautiful," she stuttered. "Where did you find these petals?"

"Thank you and that's my secret."

He left her hands and she immediately missed his touch. He pulled a chair back for her to sit. He went around to his chair after she was seated.

"I made us steak and roasted vegetables. Enjoy JJ."

"Let's eat."

They both dug in.

"This is really good, Jaxon," she said with a mouth full of vegetables.

Jessa was thankful for Lysa the ex. Without her, this scrumptious meal would not have been possible. She took a bite out of her steak and her taste buds smiled and danced happily.

"Why do you call me JJ, instead of Jessa?" she asked. She had always been curious about the nickname. Nobody except him called her that.

"You haven't figured it out yet?" He asked, a glint of mischief in his eyes.

She found herself fully curious now. She had never given much thought to the nickname and had hated it when he called her that. It didn't matter how many times she ignored him when he called her JJ or threatened to never speak to him again; he kept at it.

"I haven't actually. Can you just tell me?" She knew her voice came out whinier than firm.

The sound of his laughter was deep, guttural and he looked more beautiful laughing like that. She was not sure she would ever tell him how beautiful she thought he looked.

"I can't. It will be more fun if you figured it out." He winked.

"I am not above begging and nagging you to death, till I get my answers."

"Give it your best shot, Mrs. Jamison." He let out a cocky smile. She rolled her eyes because she knew he wouldn't budge. *Finding the reason behind his nickname for me wasn't important anyway,* she lied to herself.

"Want a slice of chocolate cake?" she asked to change the subject.

"Sure."

She went to the oven and brought out the cake she had baked in the morning. It looked moist and soft, and tasty. She may not be the best cook, but no one matched her skills in the pastry and bread making department.

Jaxon

That evening, Jaxon lay on the sofa bed in the living room. As usual, he was restless. He missed his California king bed. It was now Sunday evening and his third night under the same roof with a beautiful wife that he could not touch.

Unexpressed feelings lay bottled up in his chest. He was not sure it was wise to take the risk and reveal how he truly felt about her. What if he told her and she didn't feel the same way?

Today she had asked him about the nickname he had given her and though he was tempted to reveal the origins of the name, something held him back. He didn't think she was ready to hear what he had to say. He hoped she would figure it out soon. He had given her a clue but she missed it. As smart as she was, she was probably thinking it was something that needed decoding. He had faith in her.

He turned to the other side of the bed and wondered what they would be doing now if she was lying on this same bed with him. She seemed to be fighting hard against giving in to him. He could respect that. He liked that she wasn't easy and led by her desires.

The mixed signals she gave off were enough to fry any cable. He was sure that she would come around. But that did not stop his restlessness. He wondered what Jessa thought of him. Did she find him handsome? He knew he looked good and carried himself well, but what if he wasn't her type? *Then she'll have to make me her type,* he thought cynically.

She was the biggest tease though. She walked around the apartment in short black tights and shirts, without a bra. Nothing was left to the imagination. He could see the outline of her body perfectly. Was she oblivious to the effect she had on him?

He needed to get his mind off of *JJ.* This morning, he had called his father, even though he was supposed to yesterday. The old man was very much the same sad man he grew up with. His father assured him that he had enough food and he still had power in his home. Jaxon was grateful for that. His dad was older and needed the luxury of heat. In addition to that, his stove ran on electricity.

His train of thought was disrupted by a noise. Singing perhaps. He raised his head and could finally make out the sound clearly. It was country music seeping through the doorway. It started low, then whoever was listening to that trash increased the volume.

"What the hell."

He was not a fan of country music at all. To him it was filled with sadness and broken hearts.

He got up and walked toward the sound. The music was not letting up and he decided he had to do something to make this suffering go away. If it was a radio station, he was going to change it to something else. It would be better to hear two uninformed presenters arguing about politics than to keep listening to country music.

He walked down the short hallway and was surprised to find it coming from JJ's room. He would not have taken her as someone who loved country music. She seemed more like the jazz type. *Whatever that was.*

He pushed her door open and stood at the threshold. He wanted to close her door and scramble back, but the look on Jessa's face stopped him. She looked so peaceful, dancing to the slow rhythm of the country music in her lingerie. She looked like the goddess of slow rhythmic sex or something and Jaxon found himself pinned to a spot. His mouth became extremely dry and his heart became erratic. He could not move even if he were pushed by a bulldozer.

This was the first time he was seeing her in this state of undress and by everything that was pleasurable, he loved what he saw. Long legs, smooth skin, confidence. All he thought of as he stood there was for a chance to run his hands along the expanse of her skin. Her eyes were shut and her lips moved along with the lyrics of the song.

He would never think of country music in the same way again, not after seeing this. Her lips appealed to him, drawing him like a magnet. He wondered how they would look moaning his name.

JJ looked over and saw him standing by the door. Her eyes took him in lazily, like he was just part of the furniture, and she continued dancing. He was stunned. He did not know what to do. He expected some kind of reaction but got nothing. She did not seem to care about him seeing her practically naked. If he knew country music had this effect on her, he would have used it against her defenses earlier.

Jaxon decided that he needed to give her privacy and return to his bed. He still stood there, unable to move an inch, caught in a spell. The way Jessa's waist moved began to arouse him. He tried to think of something else.

He thought of his damaged car, then his father, yet his mind kept drawing him back to the presence in front of him. She beckoned him to come to her. He didn't stop to think of anything else. His legs dragged him along toward her.

"You're a great dancer." His voice was hoarse.

"Shhhhh," Jessa cooed, placing a hand on his lips. "Don't talk. Dance with me."

He complied, and placed his arms around her waist. After a few missteps, he followed her lead. They were so closely linked together that he caught the faint scent of lavender on her skin. He got into the rhythm, enjoying the feel of her so close to him. He wore only a pair of boxers, so her skin was against his. He still found the music terrible, but not as terrible as he thought before.

Her eyes were on his, burning with intensity, searing through his body. He had never felt so exposed and so shy before. She looked at him like she wanted to eat him up.

""Don't take your hands off my heart", by Dawn Sears," she said, "my favorite.

It describes how I am feeling right now."

"I can see why," he lied. The only thing he could see was her. He prayed for a modicum of control.

"I love country music," Jessa said again.

They continued dancing, letting only the music envelope them with her clinging onto him. Every so often, she pressed against his hardness and he swore he could see what looked like a mischievous grin forming on her face.

"You feel this song, you don't sing it," Jessa continued.

Jaxon was feeling something alright, but it was not the music. He did not know if he would ever be able to feel any music, not with Jessa pressed against his body in her lingerie.

She looked up at him with lazy eyes, stood on her tiptoes to meet him and drew his head down toward her. Their lips met in a frenzied dance. Her lips were soft and demanding. He began pushing her backward until her back was against the wall. He broke the kiss and looked down at her. She was all he wanted, but he also wanted to know she was okay with it. Her eyes told him something he had waited for long to hear. They said *fuck me*, but he had to be sure.

"Are you sure?" He waited for what felt like eternity for her response. He could see different emotions flickering through her face until she nodded.

He groaned, trying so hard to control his urges. Her needs had to come first. She was a priority. "I'm going to need actual words, my love."

"I want you," she breathed out. That was all the confirmation he needed.

He pulled down her bra and he bent his head to capture a freed nipple between his lips while his hands worked on unhooking her bra. He nibbled and sucked on it, going back and forth between right and left breasts. Her fingers brushed through his hair as her moans filled the bedroom.

He knelt in front of her and placed her right leg on top of his left shoulder. His tongue grazed her heated core through her lace underwear and she shrieked. He smelled the muskiness of her wetness. Without wasting any more time, he pulled at her underwear until it tore and threw it aside. He was now face to face with her pleasure spot. He placed her other leg over his shoulder and then flipped her again.

She gasped and he reassured her that he would not hurt her. He wrapped his arms tightly around her.

He was holding her upside down and her face was aligned to his shaft. He felt her pull his boxers down and he smirked.

Putting his tongue to work, he lapped on her pleasure spot and she gasped again. She shuddered as she released a low cry of pleasure, but she failed. Her hips moved violently as she tried to get enough of Jaxon's tongue. Her voice, which was supposed to be a low cry suddenly turned into a scream as Jaxon continued to drive her crazy.

Jessa

❧

J essa kissed his tip before her lips finally encircled it. She heard him grunt lowly. She loved the way he had made her feel some seconds ago, he even still made her feel good but she couldn't let him have all the fun. She slurped on his full length and felt him shudder. His feet started moving and soon they were both on the bed, with her on top of him.

She didn't stop. She stroked, and then licked. She could feel him jerking and she loved it even more when he started helping her fix her hair.

"Damn, J!" he let out and she smiled as she took him in, till her eyes felt watery. She choked on his full length.

"Easy girl." He continued to hold her hair from getting in her face.

She looked up at him, maintaining eye contact as she worked. He lost by closing his eyes when she paid more attention to his lower region. She began using more of her hands on his full length, stroking in spiral patterns as his tip was buried in her cute little mouth.

When she was done sending him almost over the edge, she reached for the drawer and grabbed a condom. She tore it easily and placed it on his rock hard member.

She had no idea where this new found confidence she was showing was emanating from, or what was causing it. She climbed Jaxon and hovered her heated core over his length. Slowly, she slid down him, swallowing him up. As she felt herself stretching out, she threw her head back in pleasure.

"Fuck! You're super tight," he said, grabbing her waist and pushing her down.

"You're not exactly small," came her breathy reply. They both burst out laughing hard at her comment.

A brief moment of silence passed as they both got accustomed to the other. When Jaxon spoke again, his voice was laced with pure concern. "Are you okay?" he asked.

She loved how caring he was even in the middle of their embrace. She nodded and then began to move up and down at a very slow rhythm as she placed her hands on his chest for support. She threw her head back as she began to move faster.

She bit her lower lips trying to conceal her moans but failing again. She couldn't hold it in any longer when he moved his hips to meet hers in a quick motion. Jessa screamed out.

She bent toward him, grabbed his nipples between her teeth and began biting on them ever so softly as she increased her pace. He reached for her hips and began to help her as he easily lifted her up and down on his shaft. Their erratic breathing coupled with grunts and moans filled the room blending easily with the slapping of skin against one another.

She felt so close to her climax. Her mind raced and her lips screamed without her brain even taking charge again. She trembled. "Shit, I'm cummin." She couldn't complete it as she felt her eyes roll to the back of her head.

"Fuck!" Jaxon cursed as he came to his own release.

They both stayed in that position trying to calm their breathing. After a moment, she rolled over to lie beside him. He got up and went to the washroom. When he returned, he lay down beside her and pulled her to him. She placed her head on his chest and he kissed her head and placed his leg over hers.

She looked up at his face and noticed the small smile that was beginning to play on his lips.

"What is it?" she asked as she began to trail lines on his chest with her index finger.

"I'm too mind blown to talk right now. Are you tired?"

"I'm not," she whispered then reached up to take his lips. The kiss was unrushed. She untangled her lips from his and went to his neck, biting and licking him. He drew a breath and she smiled, going down to take his nipples. She nibbled for a while, then looked up at her Jaxon and finally said, "We're just getting started."

With those words birthed from her mouth, he flipped her over and she landed on her fours giggling like a schoolgirl. He made her feel tiny, safe. She heard his intake of breath and knew exactly what he found. She made a move to turn and face him but he held her in place.

She turned shyly back at him. "It was something stupid I did when I was sixteen. No one knows except Jasmine and Meesha." During her teen years, she wanted to do something shocking and she did. She got her name tattooed in Chinese letters on her lower back. Her biggest regret ever. After it was done, she'd learn that tattoos in the location of hers were referred to as trump stamps. She had been mortified ever since and wore dresses to cover it up.

"I like it." He bent to plant a kiss on the tattoo and on each of her ass cheeks. Without warning, he drove into her and she screamed out in surprise. It soon gave way to the pleasure she felt.

She arched her back more as he stroked her faster. The bed made creaking sounds and she grabbed on to her sheets. She was being loud, and she didn't care who heard what was happening in her apartment. She wanted to get to that blissful place that only Jaxon could transport her to. His movement became erratic and she felt herself reaching that pinnacle. She screamed and spasmed all over him.

"Damn! Your body was made for mine," he said before he pulled out and poured his seed over her ass.

She slumped on the bed trying to catch her breath. Something cold was on her back and when she looked back, Jaxon was cleaning her with a washcloth. Grateful for his thoughtfulness, she smiled at him and thanked him. She was tired and needed a break.

He lay down next to her and pulled her still nude body to his warm one. She threw her arm over his chest and snuggled closer to him. She didn't know for how much longer he would be here with her but knew that this would soon come to an end.

After a while she spoke. She didn't know how to broach what was on her mind, but she decided to just say it.

"We just had unprotected sex."

"I know, I'm sorry. You have nothing to worry about. I had my last physical two weeks ago and everything was good."

"That's good to know. I'm clean too. I think this is the first time I've had sex without a condom." And it had been a while since she was intimate with a man.

"Really? That's good to know," he said, and brushed his lips on her head.

"I'm not on the pill either, so hopefully," she paused and reached out and grabbed her phone from her bedside table. She thanked God she had two fully charged portable chargers that allowed her to keep her phone and Jaxon's powered throughout this storm. She went through her phone and found the app she was looking for. "We're safe; I am not ovulating."

"We would be safe even if you weren't ovulating. I pulled out, remember?"

"Pshhh, like that's reliable birth control. Precum can also impregnate women." She felt him stiffen and turned to look into his eyes. They were hard and free of the amusing glint that resided in his eyes. "What's wrong?"

"Nothing."

"Liar. You're not telling me something." She replaced her phone on the side table and brought her hand to his chest and twirled her fingers through the short hairs. He moved away from her touch to sit at the edge of the bed. His back was to her. She grieved the loss of contact. When he finally spoke, his voice was strained.

"Remember Chloe?"

"Your college girlfriend?" She remembered the pretty brunette with blue eyes. They had met once at her brother's high school graduation. She had no idea why she remembered her.

"Yes her. She got pregnant during our second year of university," he started. This was the first time she had even heard about this. She didn't say anything; just waited for him to continue. "When she told me, I was shocked obviously. It wasn't something I wanted or even thought of. She told me to not worry about it. She said that she'd made up her mind to terminate the pregnancy. It wasn't part of her plans she had said and I agreed with her. It was an easy escape for me to not have to deal with it further. But as the day for the appointment came closer, my mind began to change."

"Did you tell her?"

He let out a breath. "I wanted to but I couldn't. I didn't want to be the reason she second guessed her decision. The decision was hers to make. We both had our entire lives in front of us. I accompanied her to the appointment and when it was done, she told me that the main reason for her decision was because she was unsure of who the father was. I left her at the clinic and never saw her again."

Jessa shifted and came up behind Jaxon. She lay her head on his shoulders and encircled his chest with her arms.

"I'm sorry, Jaxon." She placed a kiss on the back of his neck.

"You don't owe me an apology." He brought her hands up to his lips and kissed her knuckles.

"I know. I'm sorry you had to go through that."

"After that incident, I've been very careful. I don't want to risk it." Now she understood a little bit more. Jaxon was protecting himself. He didn't want to place himself in a situation where he wouldn't have control of the outcome. She pulled him backward till they were both lying on the bed again.

"I hate that you went through that."

"I hate that I was so naïve and reckless."

"I don't think you should beat yourself up about it. You said it yourself that it was Chloe's decision. You were supportive despite your own reservations. That's something to be proud of. You respected her decision as a woman."

She felt his smile in his next words.

"Why do I get the feeling that you're proud of me?"

"Because I am," she said, yawning. He pulled her closer to him, tilted her head and then kissed her. It was slow and sweet, unlike the kisses they shared before. Having him share something hurtful from his past made her feel closer to him. When he pulled away from the kiss, he brought her head down to his chest.

She closed her eyes and fell asleep.

When she emerged from her slumber, the room was completely dark and her back was to Jaxon's solid chest. She figured Jaxon must have put off the candle after she fell asleep. Jaxon kissed her neck, shoulders and brought his hand down to the apex of her thighs. He began stroking her with his fingers.

Though her mind was hazy from slumber, her body was fully aware of his machinations. She heard the sound of a condom opening and soon after, he lifted her leg and slipped easily into her wet core. He possessed her body, plunging into the very depths of her soul. Each stroke broke down another piece of the defenses she had against him. She surrendered to his passion easily. He brought his hand between her legs and rubbed on her sensitive nub. It threw her over the edge and she shattered around him. She felt him go deeper and he groaned and exploded inside her.

Neither shifted from their position. Jessa did not want to. She loved being connected to him the way they were. She fell asleep again.

Jaxon

J axon looked Jessa over from the window pane where he stood. "We should go for a walk."

She looked up at him from the book she was reading. "It's freezing outside. I'm not sure I want to brave the cold."

He wouldn't take no for an answer. He walked over to the sofa where she sat and took a seat. He placed his arms around her shoulder and she snuggled closer to him.

"We need some fresh air. We've been cooped up for days, not that I've minded. I want to see you in the bright light of day. We can walk to the Seven Eleven and grab a few things."

"But -."

"Sshh." He placed his index finger on her lips then placed a kiss on the top of her head. Jessa didn't grumble again; he just heard her sigh.

Some minutes later, she emerged from her room in a pink knitted sweater and tight blue jeans. She always looked beautiful.

"Ready?" he asked.

"Just as soon as I put on my gloves, scarf and coat." She opened her hallway closet and pulled out her winter outerwear. When she was done putting on her snow boots, he offered her his gloved hand. She took it easily and their fingers intertwined as they walked out the door.

She was right when she said it was freezing. The cold air hit their faces as soon as they stepped outside. Jessa used her free hand to zip up her snow coat to her neck and tightened her scarf around her neck and lower face. Jaxon was glad when he saw the guy from the other day, the one that had confessed to liking Jessa.

He lifted their interlaced fingers and brought it to his lips, Jessa unaware of the show he was trying to put on and just turned and blushed at the movement.

"I told you it was freezing. We should have stayed inside." They trudged down the street.

"Mmhh," he answered casually.

"Did I mention that I may soon be a vice principal at my school?"

"Uhmm, your brother mentioned it to me. Thought it was already a done deal?"

"Nah," she said as she shook her head. "It's not a done deal. The school board has to approve it first. I think I have a leg up since the principal vouched for me and her husband is on the board."

He pursed his lips. "Then why sound nervous about it?"

"You never know with these things." She shrugged. "They can offer the position to someone else who works for the board."

"You're smart; I doubt that would happen."

"But-" she tried to protest.

"Look," he started in an assuring voice as they rounded a corner. They could now see the store a few meters ahead. "I'm very sure you'd make the best principal. You make the best of everything. The best sister, the best friend, the best teacher, the best wife."

She scoffed, "You're just saying that to get in my pants, and it's really not working." It was working though.

"Wanna bet?" He smirked and that glint played in his eyes.

"I'm done betting with you." They both laughed.

He stopped just in front of the store, turned to look her in the eyes and cupped her face in his hand. "They'd be losing out if they picked someone else. Sure, it would take some adjustments on your end, but you'll do just fine. You haven't gotten the position and you're already concerned about messing up. You'll give it your all, JJ."

That seemed to calm her down along with the kiss he planted on her fore-head. She smiled. "You need to change professions. Jaxon the motivational speaker."

"Maybe I should." He took hold of her hand as they walked into the grocery store.

They made a quick work of the small Seven Eleven. They got frozen steaks in a box, a small case of beer and a bottle of sangria.

When they were done, they went to the counter and unloaded their items. There was a grey haired, bulky woman behind the counter.

As the woman scanned their items she spoke to them.

"You two are such a sight to see. You remind me of me and my dear husband, may his soul rest in peace." She paused and sniffed, then continued. "It's nice to see a young couple watch each other the way me and my Thomas watched each other."

Jaxon tightened his hold on Jessa, "She's my wife. I only have eyes for her. And please accept my sympathy."

He felt when Jessa stiffened. He drew small circles in her palms and smiled at her.

The cashier nodded, "Thank you Dear."

Jaxon paid the cashier and walked out of the store with Jessa. They walked back to her condo in comfortable silence.

When they arrived, she hurried to her room to change while he stayed in the kitchen and grilled the steak. While they ate the meal he prepared, they discussed varying topics. Jaxon told her about the new game he and his partners were developing and also about them branching out to Europe. Jessa told him about the trip she had planned for the summer to Venice and about her concern for her father, who won't take it easy despite doctor's orders. They laughed and talked. Jaxon couldn't remember the last time he felt more at ease.

Jaxon

When they were done eating, Jessa pushed her chair back and began gathering the dirty plates. She placed the plates in the sink as Jaxon hunched over the fridge, trying to decide what to drink. The meal he prepared was delicious and the conversation that ensued between them was refreshing.

"Can you show me how to play one of your games?" The electricity had returned earlier today and she knew that their time together would soon come to an end. Roads were already being cleared.

He looked at her, like he was trying to decide if she was messing with him or not.

"You?"

She rolled her eyes. "I asked, didn't I?"

"Alright. Go to the living room, I'll show you." He disappeared down her hallway. Her brother had bought her a PlayStation last Christmas. He said it was for her to play games, but she knew he bought it for when he came over to her home.

She got comfortable on the couch and reappeared with his laptop. He sat next to her and his cologne assuaged her nerves. She wanted to forget the game and make out with him. It took him a while to set it up, and as he did, he answered her questions.

"How come we can't play it on the PS4?"

"The game is still in development. It's not on PlayStations yet."

"Oh, cool."

When the game loaded, he shifted the laptop so that she could see what was happening on the screen. She leaned in closer to him and she heard his deep intake of breath as his hand shook.

"Show me how to play."

He did. He explained the game to her and showed her what buttons to press. Not once did he become impatient or annoyed with her questioning. Soon they were both engrossed in the game.

"I want to go again; I'm sure I can beat you," she said enthusiastically.

After three whole rounds, she still did not beat him. Her fingers became tired, and though she wished to win, she knew she couldn't play anymore.

"This isn't over," she said, dropping the wireless mouse and slumping into her chair.

He chuckled. She finally understood how he made so much money. His game was one of the most addictive things she had come across. Jaxon, along with her brother and Antonio were brilliant. They spent enough time playing video games in their youth to know what would sell.

She glanced at him for a second. She liked how his smiles always reached his eyes and how they twinkled when he became competitive. He made her laugh and challenged her. She feared putting her heart out on the line for him. Her brother and his friends changed girlfriends as often as they changed underwear. She wouldn't end up heartbroken over him. They were too intricately linked with family and friends. What happened between them needed to remain casual.

She closed her eyes and shook the thoughts away. He held her by the waist and lifted her unto his lap. She straddled him.

He easily lifted her up and placed her back on the couch, with him being on top. She wrapped her legs around him as her hands drew a map on his body. She didn't know when she'd ever get used to his lips on hers, her body in his, them being one. She loved how perfectly they fit each other. No one had ever made her feel the way he did and she liked it that way. She didn't want another, just him.

As they both went on a rapturous journey that night, bringing each other to heights never experienced before, she stopped thinking. She only lived in the moment, with his domineering strokes and demanding kisses. The marriage, her past and her future unthought of.

At some point during their sexual escapade, they ended up on the floor wrapped up in each other's arms.

"You awake?" He asked in the silence.

"Yup," she replied, popping the p.

"Is your favorite color still blue?"

She was confused. "How did you… never mind. Yes, it is. Is yours still green?"

He quirked a brow. "Green was never my favorite color." He smiled. "I see what you're doing."

She smiled coyly. "I assumed your favorite color like you assumed mine." She shrugged her shoulders.

He pulled her closer.

"I didn't assume. I know a lot about you. Like how your beautiful brown skin turns a shade darker in the summer, and how you become flushed when I speak to you like I'm speaking now, soft and low. I know that you prefer to get your hair braided during the summer and wear it straight during the colder months." He trailed a finger down her spine, and she swallowed a lump that had formed in her throat. "I know that you prefer dresses over jeans and that you love your friends and family. You would give them the clothes of your back if you had to. To answer your question, my favorite color used to be the color of your eyes; now it's the color of your eyes when you climax with me inside you."

She did not know what to say after all he said. She felt her heartbeat between her legs and she crossed them. She was unaware of him watching her all this time.

"You're not a stalker are you?" she asked jokingly even though she felt not one bit of humor.

"I'm just very observant."

"You claim to know a lot about me so I'm gonna quiz you."

He smirked. "Hopefully this quiz doesn't end with us trying to fly off your balcony."

"Ouch," he said, after she pinched him under the covers.

"Let's begin –"

He cut her off. "Wait. What do I get for participating in this quiz? The last time I played one of you games, I ended up married. What prize could you offer that would top that?"

She rolled her eyes. When he said stuff like that it made her think of the future. Their future. Living together as man and wife and having good days as they have had for the past few days. She didn't want to think about that.

"I can only offer kisses. Take it or leave it."

"I take it. I'll even be presumptuous and collect my prize early." Before she could protest, his lips came crashing down on hers and his tongue invaded her open mouth. The passion in the kiss shocked her. It stole her breath away and she surrendered to it. When he finally pulled away, they were both breathless.

"That's cheating," she finally said when she was able to catch her breath.

"No, it's called having faith in myself and my abilities. Now we can argue about me claiming my prize early or you can try to prove me wrong."

She took a moment to think and finally asked, "What's my dream car?"

"Hmmm. A Range Rover. You asked your parents for one on your sixteenth birthday and was sorely disappointed by the Toyota sitting in your driveway." He chuckled.

She remembered that day. She had been so sure they would have gotten her a Range Rover; after all she was their only daughter and they should want to make her happy. At her disappointment, her dad had suggested returning the car and she had puckered up and accepted the offending gift. That car served her for six years before it got totaled.

"That one was easy. Everyone knows that about me. If I get the VP position, I'll finally get one."

"We're married now. You know you can afford to get one delivered to you next week if you wanted."

"Jaxon."

"You want to be independent and get it on your own. Admirable."

That's not what she had intended to say. She wanted to remind him that their marriage was not real and she had no rights over his money.

"Next question. How many kids do I want?"

"Tough one, but I'll say three. You do work in a school and I know you love kids."

"That, Mr. Jamison, is incorrect." She giggled. "I love kids, but I'm scared of childbirth."

He stared, and she continued.

"If I'm ever lucky enough to fall head over heels with a man who wants kids, I may just have one. Two max, if he is good with the first. If not, I'm perfectly okay with becoming a spinster."

"A what?"

"A spinster is a woman who never married or has kids."

"That's impossible now isn't it? You're married."

"For now," she said softly, although she was no longer sure. She decided to bring the subject back to safe ground. "How many kids do you want?"

"A house full. Four or five. I want a busy household." She suddenly remembered that he was an only child. It must have been quiet in his house, with no siblings."

"Is being an only child the only thing encouraging your decision for a large family?" She looked up at him.

"Not fully." He paused. "I loved being the center of my parent's attention. I was all they had and they gave me their all. Kids need that. After my mom passed away, my dad changed. I wish I had siblings at the time. Someone to understand what I was going through when my dad became reserved. I'm worried about him. He isn't living. He's surviving. I wonder sometimes if he blames me for my mom's death."

"Hey." She sat up to look at his face. "I'm sure he doesn't blame you."

"I am to blame though. She got accepted into a new trial but refused to go. She wanted to spend her last few months with me and dad. Dad begged her to go to the trial. It would have lasted a year."

"Listen to me; you are not to blame and if your dad blames you, that's on him. Your mom was a grown woman and she made her decision. She wanted to spend it with her family. We can't fault her for that, and you shouldn't blame yourself either."

He nodded, and then looked hard and long at her. His voice softened. "Jessa, we need to talk about our marriage."

"Let's not tonight." She tilted her head up and kissed him. At that moment, she knew she had fallen in love with Jaxon, her husband.

Jaxon

〜⚬⚬⚬〜

*T*he morning was bright, and skies cleared. Plow trucks could be heard outside clearing up the snow. It had been almost a week since Jaxon was stuck in Jessa's house. Now, as he looked through the window, he was grateful that he came over to Jessa's last week. He was even more grateful that she had let him into her house and bed.

For the past two days since baring out his family problems they had done little else but made love to each other and talk. They had shared a lot. Jaxon had felt the spark in his soul, this fire that had come on just recently because of this woman he was very much in love with.

He watched her sleeping on the bed beside him and knew that he had made no mistake. Everything he wanted in a woman had been delivered to him in an attractive package and he would be mad if he let that slip from him. Her eye lashes lapped on her eye lids, she breathed slowly and gracefully. She was curled up due to the cold weather. He covered her slender legs with the blanket and she stirred a little.

The more he watched her, the more his boner grew. His heart was also expanding like it was as flexible as his member. He wanted this woman, needed her even. He did not want it to be just a dream from which he would wake up and be left with nothing more than memories. He was certain that even in old age, they would lie together with him still looking lovingly at her, reminiscing on their youth and the many stupid things they would have done together.

He could almost imagine it, them both on the bed. Her hands clasped and holding her head as she stared at home with that playful grin spread across her lips, he reaching out for her face and touching it. She closing her eyes at the feel of his fingers.

Something was on his mind however. All through the time they had stayed together, they had never discussed their marriage - instead she had always shut him down. He needed to know where exactly he stood with her.

His eyes took in her sleeping figure again. She looked peaceful and he could stare at her for days. It was a thing of surprise that this body had enough to command his attention for as long as she wanted.

He waited for her to stir and look at him. There was a smile in place, waiting for her. She opened her eyes and she didn't smile at him; she grinned at him.

"Good morning, Baby," he greeted.

"I can't remember you waking up this early," she commented.

"Me neither," he said thoughtfully.

His thoughts got away from him. Jaxon had done many things before but this was difficult. Thinking of doing something was way easier than actually doing it. He studied her angelic features. Her brown skin turned a bit pink under his intense stare, if that was even possible.

"Did you sleep well?" He asked.

"You know I didn't," she responded with a knowing look on her face. "You barely let me close my eyes."

"You beg and I deliver," he said simply and winked, slapping her butt. She hit him with a pillow. He caught it easily and flung it away, their laughter filling the room. He placed his hands on her leg and stared at her, a look of seriousness passing his face. "Hey, Jessa, I want to talk to you about something," he said.

"What is it?" She tried to sit up. His hands still rested comfortably on her legs.

"Let's make this marriage permanent. Let's move in together."

Silence.

She looked like she was going to say something but then her lips didn't move. When he felt like she was not going to comment, she finally did.

"Where is this coming from?" Her voice was tender, her eyes were confused and she had stiffened.

"We're married. And I know we did not get married under the best circumstances, but we can make something great out of this marriage. We've known each other for a long time and we're really great in bed together."

She shook her head clearly disagreeing with him. "That isn't enough to make a marriage work, Jaxon. Sex isn't what keeps marriages going. It's a lot more than a few rounds of fucking."

"The past few days have shown us how deeply we care for each other." She was still shaking her head, he continued. "I'm sure we can work this out. We have something beautiful."

"Caring deeply is not enough either. Marriages deserve love and support from each other," she said. She shrugged the blanket that covered her bare legs, grabbed the robe she had discarded on the floor then covered up. She stood up and walked toward the door.

He followed her to the kitchen, his heart in his hand. She filled her cup with water from the tap.

"I know all of that JJ. I love you. We can make this thing work between us."

"This is all too sudden." She drank the water and dropped the cup. "It's too much," she said as she gathered her robe more, wrapping her arms around her body.

"How is it sudden? I have loved you for years. The past week with you only solidified that love." His voice was pleading with her but she wasn't looking like she would budge.

"Please stop. I can't deal with this now. Just stop!" She turned away from him and held the sink.

"If you need space to decide then I can give it to you." He walked to meet her and placed his hands on her shoulder. For a second, it seemed like she relaxed into his touch but then, she shrugged and pushed his hands away. They fell limply to his side. She still didn't turn to look at him.

"I don't need space. I've made up my mind. I want you out of my home and I want an annulment." Her voice was stern.

He sighed and walked back to her room. He would give her time. He refused to believe that this was the end of it all. Dumping everything on her so soon made her retract. He couldn't blame her.

He got dressed quickly and packed up his gym bag with his belongings. Everything he touched reminded him of her. Her scent had been imprinted on all of his belongings. His mind only sought for her. His body needed her and his heart felt like it would crash any minute soon.

When he was done, he walked back to the kitchen to meet her still standing by the sink. She looked down at her fingers, not even sparing him a glance.

'I'm going home," he said.

Jessa never acknowledged him. He took one last look at her, then walked away.

Jessa

essa stood before the mirror, staring at her outfit. She felt beautiful. It had been almost two weeks since Jaxon had walked out of her life. She missed him so much that it hurt when she thought of him. Her heart felt like it was shattered in pieces.

She wished she could turn back the clock and accept his preposition. She did not want to live without him but it was too late. She had tried calling him all to no avail. The calls always ended up with his voicemail. It's ironic that he was the one dodging her calls now. Her heart felt hollow and nothing could bring her joy or brighten her spirits. Not even the letter she had received appointing her the new vice principal of her school. Thoughts of him and the short time they spent together plagued her mind.

It didn't help that he had been in her apartment, it didn't help that she had to sleep on the same bed in which they'd made love. It didn't help that she had tried to cook really nice meals like him but had failed. He had walked away from her with her heart in his hand. Nothing seemed to be helping these days.

She felt like the girl Rhonda Vincent sang about in her song "Once a Day".

After she pulled down on her peach floral dress since it rode up quite a bit. Her eyes lingered on an envelope Jaxon had sent containing documents that would free her from their faux pas in Vegas. On the envelope he wrote, *What happens in Vegas, stays in Vegas.* She swallowed and her mouth felt dry.

She had believed that this was what she wanted and could not wait to get her hands on it, but the day she received it, she felt something die within her. She studied her sad face in the mirror before smiling. That was the mask she would plaster on her face for Meesha and Connor's couple's party.

She went down to the garage for her car and made her way to the venue. The roads were almost empty and she got there on time.

"Jessa!" Meesha screamed when she saw her walking toward the reception.

Jessa ran into Meesha's arms before turning to hug Jasmine and Connor. The couple hurried away to welcome other guests after a little catching up.

"How are you girl?" Jasmine asked.

"I'm okay," she replied.

Jasmine was glowing herself. If she was a man, Jasmine would have been her type of woman. She had thick curly hair, a ready smile and she was intelligent.

"Haven't really heard from you for some time now. We were worried."

"I was just busy with school. The blizzard caused some missed school days and I have been trying to get my students all caught up."

Jasmine turned to look at her. She was trying too hard to appear happy and was failing woefully. She looked away suddenly feeling like her friend would see right through her smile and her eyes fell on Jaxon. He was sitting beside a woman and they were cozy.

"Who's that with Jaxon?" She asked Jasmine trying her best to sound as casual as she could.

"Who?" Jasmine followed her friend's eyes.

"The woman in that too short black dress."

"His date, I believe," she said and sipped her drink. "I think her name is Lysa or something."

Her heart plummeted. Could that be the chef Jasmine had probably gotten the names mixed up. She bit her lip a little bit too harshly as she saw their interlocked fingers.

Didn't he say it didn't work out because he was in love with someone else?

She sighed as the anger began to build up steadily in her heart.

"Why's she touching him like that?" she asked, her voice cold.

Jasmine looked at her friend with concern.

"Why do you care? Is there something going on that I don't know about?"

Jessa ignored her friend for a second as she grabbed a glass of champagne from a waiter, gulped it at once then turned to her friend. "Yes. He is my husband." She placed the empty glass back on the waiter's tray and managed to throw him a, "thank you".

She did not stop to think about it. She walked to the podium unaware of her friend's shocked countenance at her announcement. With her head up, and her stance unwavering, she finally made it there and grabbed the microphone. Without pausing, or having a second thought, she broke into her favorite country song by Dawn Sears.

The guests all stopped what they were doing and openly gaped at her. She didn't care, didn't want to care. Her focus was on her husband. Even though she was off key, there was something enthralling about her voice. Soon the band joined in, backing her up. The more she sang, the closer she moved to Jaxon.

Finally, she stood before him. Her pride was out of the door by now.

It had taken her a lot to come to this point. Overcoming the fear she had about trusting him, trusting he would say "yes" when she asked him to take her back. She had pushed aside the thought of whatever anger or regret her parents would feel when they heard their daughter got married in Vegas while she was drunk.

"I'm sorry," she said, standing before him and totally ignoring the other woman. "I should not have doubted you," she said, with tears streaming down her face now. She sobbed.

There was no emotion on Jaxon's face. He gave her nothing, but she went on.

"I love you, Jaxon," she said. "I want to be your wife, forever. I don't care that we got married in Vegas while we were extremely drunk. I am glad that I did it with you. The thought of not spending the rest of my life with you fills me with nothing but dread. Please forgive me."

"Why are you doing this here? Now?"

"I love our banter, I love how safe you make me feel. I love how your eyes twinkle at the corners when you're excited. I love waking up to your tender kisses and your, your," she looked around and noticed her brother in the corner and she swallowed, "you know what." Jaxon's lips twitched. "I love you and you've become my entire world." She placed the microphone down when she realized everyone had heard her confession. Anything else she needed to say, didn't need to be heard by everyone.

He took her hand in his, rubbed circles with his thumb and that seemed to help her calm down a bit. "A future without my JJ, is not a future at all," he finally said and her heart did a summersault.

"Really?"

"Do you even have to ask? I have been intrigued with you since you were seventeen. I've watched you and waited for you to finally notice me. I'm glad you finally came to your senses." He kissed her.

"I'm sorry it took me so long."

"You don't need to apologize, JJ."

"I finally figured it out."

"What?"

"My nickname. You've been calling me Jessa Jamison for years?"

"If you want something as badly as I wanted you, you put it out there in the universe Mrs. Jamison."

"How soon do you think I can make it official?" She wanted to change her name as soon as possible.

"As soon as you want, JJ."

"I love you Mr. Jamison."

"I love you more Baby," he said, his voice barely above a hoarse whisper.

She pressed her lips up to meet his inviting ones and they were both swept away in a world of passion known to only them.

The crowd erupted in applause, but Jaxon obviously wasn't done. He reached into his jacket pocket, not losing eye contact with his woman, he got in one knee and pulled out a ring.

"I know we're already married but I never got the chance to ask you. JJ, the week I spent with you were the best days of my entire adult life. I wanna have many more of those days with you by my side. Will you marry me?" He asked with that smirk on his face. The smirk she had always wanted to wipe off, today, she understood that it was meant only for her.

"Yes! I'll marry you and move in with you!"

He got up and slid the ring onto her finger. She was his, and he was hers, to hold, for better or for worse, in sickness and in health, till death did them part. Her heart swelled with joy at the realization that he was hers.

Their lips met and he tasted the saltines of her tears. She wrapped her arms around his neck and he picked her up, holding her waist and twirling her as their lips continued to move in sync with the other. When they pulled apart, he leaned in and licked her tears. This time, the kiss was chaste.

The clapping came again reminding them of the crowd that had encircled them.

Jessa felt guilty as she glanced briefly at her friends. They along with her family appeared the most shocked in the whole room. She knew they would give her hell for keeping the marriage a secret, but they would get over it.

She hadn't realized when the woman who was hanging on to Jaxon disappeared. She turned her gaze back to the man who still held her in his arms, her husband, all hers. Her parents and brother came forward to talk to them. She assured them that she would explain everything after the party.

She didn't feel the need to explain her decision because all that mattered were, she, Jaxon and their future. Despite this, she knew she owed them all and explanation.

"A toast! To our newest couple!" Connor shouted above the applause and everyone rose their glasses in the air.

Epilogue

J essa was standing in the window of the nursery, looking out, with a drink in her hand. She turned from the window to see Jaxon cradling their newborn baby son, Vega. There was satisfaction on his face. It reflected what she felt about herself, about him, about their family. Her hands fidgeted with the ring on her finger while she watched Jaxon. It was a pastime of hers.

She and Jaxon had bought a house in Kingston after she became pregnant. Before that, they lived in her condo on weekdays and on the weekends and school breaks they spent in his condo in Toronto.

He had decided to begin working from home so he could look after their child and any other children they wanted to have in the future. He was able to do so easily since he was his own boss and his company could be run from anywhere. They hired a nanny for the days Jaxon may need to be out of town, or for their occasional date nights or spur of the moment getaways. He wanted Jessa to pursue her career. Jessa could not believe her luck. It was as if Jaxon was just made for her. She walked over to where her family sat and tilted her husband's head backward to plant some kisses on his lips.

"Thanks JJ," her husband said smiling. She knew he was thanking her for more than just the kisses. She smiled with satisfaction then planted another kiss on her son's forehead.

"I'll be in the room Babe," she said then winked at him.

Jaxon didn't miss the movement of when her lower lips got tucked in between her teeth. Her hips swayed and just before she disappeared down the passage, she said, "I'll be up waiting for you in bed."

Sure enough, she was waiting for him. After tucking in their son for the night, he met her standing and looking herself over in the full-length mirror. He moved to stand behind her and took hold of her hips.

"JJ." His hot breath fanned her neck. Then he planted a kiss on her earlobe. His hands easily snaked its way around her tiny waist. "You look good enough to devour."

She smiled sweetly. Her right hand reached for his neck and she relaxed into him. They stayed in that position for a while, as she thought of how lucky she was to have him and him.

She remembered the dinner he had prepared this evening. She remembered how they would both hurl up in the kitchen when she was doing the dishes, discussing and playing with water. How Vega would be placed in his playpen and they'd steal kisses from each other. She ran through what her life had become, and she was more than pleased.

Jaxon was the first to open his eyes. He reached for the hem of her night gown and tried to lift it up. She giggled and placed her free hand on his, stopping him. He bit on her ear lobe and she shrieked. His hands roamed her soft skin.

He continued his journey, not once looking elsewhere but only at her eyes through the mirror. He was successful in lifting her silk nightwear completely, leaving her bare. His eyes did a slow perusal of her body. It sent tingles down to her womb.

"You like what you see?" She quirked her brow and grinned.

He turned her to face him, then planted a kiss on her lips, her cheeks, her forehead and her lips again. "Very much. I'm never going to get tired of looking at you." She tried to suppress another smile, she didn't want him to get tired either.

He lifted her up in bridal style, her back landed softly on the bed and he positioned himself in between her legs. He looked down at her before moving down to meet her thighs. He carried her right leg up and planted it on his shoulder as he began to leave trails of kisses. Sweet, tender kisses, until he reached her clit.

He smelled her arousal and with no warning, he began to slurp on her clitoris. He knew he was doing well when she reached for his head and pushed him deeper into her.

He stopped without warning, just like he'd started.

"What's wrong?" she asked, a little but frustrated.

"I want you to sit on my face. I want you to ride my face babe."

His words had shocked her and she didn't do much to hide it. And she did get on top of his face using the edge of the bed as support.

His lips began his sexual assault on her.

"Fuck!" she cussed as she began rocking his face violently. She couldn't hold it in. She wasn't trying to hold it in. She moved her hips and screamed in pleasure. It didn't take long for her to explode.

Her legs wobbled as she moved from his face to the bed. She was breathless and exhausted. Jaxon was just getting started. When she opened her eyes, she saw him naked. He moved to her and stretched her legs open.

She didn't have time to process what was about to happen as his length stretched her slowly. He began to move at a very even pace, giving her time to recover but not completely. He used his hands to tuck her loose hair behind her ear.

"I love you," she declared when she could finally form coherent words.

"I love you even more." He kissed her. "Want me to speed things up a bit?"

"I always do."

In that moment, as she bucked her hips to meet his hard thrust. With her nails biting into the skin of his back, and her legs caged him from withdrawing completely, he remembered how lucky he was. Her soft moans filled his ears as she came crashing again, shaking beneath him. With one last thrust, he too came.

They looked at each other with mischievous gleams, knowing what the other thought. They both covered their mouths, stifling their laughers. They hoped they didn't wake their son up.

"I'm so glad we married in Vegas." Going down to the bar on that night was the best thing to ever happen to her.

"Me too, Darling," he responded.

"One more round?" she asked seductively.

"I thought you'd never ask."

Other Books By The Author

Stand Alone titles

Sold To The Highest Bidder

Desperate to buy the bakery where she slaved over for years, Nazalie decides to auction off the only thing she owns that is worth something: Her virginity.

My Wife's Baby

An unplanned pregnancy leads a young couple down a dark path, which leaves them reeling when they find out the truth behind the origins of the pregnancy.

Anderson Sisters Series
Claiming His Wife (Anderson Sisters Book 1)

A young wife returns home with one thing on her mind. Divorce. Her husband, however, won't make it easy for her to walk away from him that easily.

Holiday Romances
Christmas Ever After

When a frightful encounter culminates into Trinity and Michael meeting, he brings forth a proposition. With Christmas on the horizon, will Trinity jump at the opportunity Michael presented her?

Manufactured by Amazon.ca
Bolton, ON

13618566R00048